And now Silhouette Romance proudly presents
WEDDING DAY BABY
by Moyra Tarling.

It's a

Bundles of Joy

SOMETIMES BIG SURPRISES COME IN SMALL PACKAGES!

Dear Reader,

Silhouette welcomes popular author Judy Christenberry to the Romance line with a touching story that will enchant readers in every age group. In *The Nine-Month Bride,* a wealthy rancher who wants an heir and a prim librarian who wants a baby marry for convenience, but imminent parenthood makes them rethink their vows....

Next, Moyra Tarling delivers the emotionally riveting BUNDLES OF JOY tale of a mother-to-be who discovers that her child's father doesn't remember his own name— let alone the night they'd created their *Wedding Day Baby.* Karen Rose Smith's miniseries DO YOU TAKE THIS STRANGER? continues with *Love, Honor and a Pregnant Bride,* in which a jaded cowboy learns an unexpected lesson in love from an expectant beauty.

Part of our MEN! promotion, *Cowboy Dad* by Robin Nicholas features a deliciously handsome, duty-minded father aiming to win the heart of a woman who's sworn off cowboys. Award-winning Marie Ferrarella launches her latest miniseries, LIKE MOTHER, LIKE DAUGHTER, with *One Plus One Makes Marriage.* Though the math sounds easy, the road to "I do" takes some emotional twists and turns for this feisty heroine and the embittered man she loves. And Romance proudly introduces Patricia Seeley, one of Silhouette's WOMEN TO WATCH. A ransom note—for a cat!—sets the stage where *The Millionaire Meets His Match.*

Hope you enjoy this month's offerings!

Mary-Theresa Hussey
Senior Editor, Silhouette Romance

Please address questions and book requests to:
Silhouette Reader Service
U.S.: 3010 Walden Ave., P.O. Box 1325, Buffalo, NY 14269
Canadian: P.O. Box 609, Fort Erie, Ont. L2A 5X3

WEDDING DAY BABY

Moyra Tarling

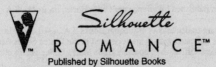

Silhouette

R O M A N C E™

Published by Silhouette Books

America's Publisher of Contemporary Romance

To Grace Green,
(The Scottish Connection)
For your friendship and support.
Thank you!

 SILHOUETTE BOOKS

ISBN 0-373-19325-4

WEDDING DAY BABY

Copyright © 1998 by Moyra Tarling

This edition published by arrangement with Harlequin Books S.A.

® and TM are trademarks of Harlequin Books S.A., used under license. Trademarks indicated with ® are registered in the United States Patent and Trademark Office, the Canadian Trade Marks Office and in other countries.

Printed in U.S.A.

Books by Moyra Tarling

Silhouette Romance

MOYRA TARLING

is the youngest of four children born and raised in Aberdeenshire, Scotland. It was there that she was first introduced to and became hooked on romance novels. After immigrating to Vancouver, Canada, Ms. Tarling met her future husband, Noel, at a party in Birch Bay— and promptly fell in love. They now have two children. Together they enjoy browsing through antique shops and auctions, looking for various items, from old gramophones to antique corkscrews and buttonhooks.

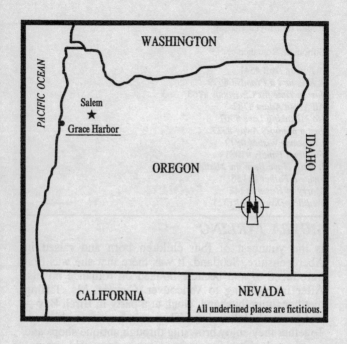

PACIFIC OCEAN

WASHINGTON

Salem
★
Grace Harbor

OREGON

IDAHO

N

CALIFORNIA

NEVADA
All underlined places are fictitious.

Prologue

Lieutenant Commander Dylan O'Connor lay on the bed staring at the sleeping figure of the young woman beside him.

He gazed intently at Maggie Fairchild, memorizing one by one each stunning feature: skin as flawless as fine porcelain, classic cheekbones, the smooth curve of her neck, the way her long, dark hair curled invitingly around her small delicate ears, and her long lashes concealing eyes the color of rich, milk chocolate.

Dylan felt the steady rhythm of his heart falter for a moment as his glance fell on the sensual fullness of Maggie's lips; lips still swollen from his kisses, lips with a taste and texture he knew he'd never forget.

The memory of her response, at once so totally innocent yet undeniably and incredibly erotic, ricocheted through him, and he felt his whole body react.

Not for the first time since he'd walked into Maggie's bedroom less than six hours ago, Dylan found himself in the grip of a desire so strong he could barely control it.

It had been a little after midnight when he'd heard the muffled sounds of crying coming from the room next door.

Throughout the double funeral service Maggie had stood by his side in silent sorrow, and he'd admired her quiet dignity, her stoic presence at a time of such profound sadness.

Together they'd suffered a devastating loss: she, the father she'd adored and he, his aunt, the only woman to breach the wall he'd built around his heart.

He'd sat down on Maggie's bed and eased her gently into his arms, stroking the silky strands of her hair and rocking her until her sobs gradually subsided.

In some strange way he'd found comfort in the very act of comforting, and when she'd lifted her head and given him a tentative smile, it had seemed the most natural thing in the world to touch his mouth to hers.

He hadn't been prepared in any way for the passion that had exploded between them like a lab experiment gone awry, igniting a need that had burned through them at lightning speed.

They'd made love with a kind of frenetic urgency, as if perhaps they were both afraid the world might suddenly come to an end.

When it was over they'd stared at each other in silent wonder before beginning the entire process again. Their second journey had been infinitely slower as they'd explored each other's bodies more thoroughly, savoring the tender touches and delighting in each other's breathless responses, as together they made the heady climb to sensual fulfillment.

Dylan slowly released the breath he was holding, fighting the urge to kiss the rosy lips and rekindle the fire he knew would quickly consume them.

The sun was making its slow ascent into the sky, and as the dawn broke, drawing shadows on the bedroom wall, for the first time in his life Dylan found himself dreaming dreams and making wishes.

His hand trembled a little as he reached out to gently finger a lock of Maggie's hair.

The strident ring of his cellular phone shattered the stillness, and as Maggie's eyes flickered open, Dylan snatched up the receiver from the bedside table.

Even before he heard the voice of his commanding officer, Dylan silently acknowledged that dreams and wishes had no place in his life...not now...maybe not ever.

Chapter One

Maggie Fairchild closed the door to Dr. Whitney's office and stood for a moment on the sidewalk enjoying the warmth of the afternoon sunshine.

The doctor had just assured her everything was fine. But Maggie couldn't seem to quell her growing apprehension about the impending birth of her baby, with her due date, June 22, less than a month away.

Drawing a deep, steadying breath, she pushed her fears aside and gently placed a hand on her swollen abdomen, smiling to herself when she felt the baby kick in instant response to her touch.

"Let's go home." She spoke the words softly, lovingly, before joining the trickle of tourists meandering down Grace Harbor's main thoroughfare.

When she reached Indigo Street, Maggie rounded the corner and collided with something warm and solid and decidedly unyielding.

"Oh!" Maggie stumbled backward, and instantly a strong pair of hands reached out to steady her.

"I'm so sorry." The deep, rich, masculine voice washed over her, and Maggie's head jerked up and her heart slammed against her rib cage in startled response when she found herself staring at the handsome, unforgettable features of Dylan O'Connor. He was the man who'd said goodbye to her eight months ago, the man she'd given up hope of ever seeing again, the man whose child lay nestled safely beneath her heart.

"Dylan?" His name came out in a breathless whisper, and Maggie felt her pulse trip over itself in alarm at the look of bewilderment she could see in the depths of his silver-gray eyes.

On hearing the woman use his name, Dylan inhaled sharply, and his gaze flew to her face. He could feel his heart pounding in his chest as he studied her shocked expression, all the while silently praying that this time his mind would relinquish just one small memory.

His doctors at the naval base in San Diego had advised against making the trip to Grace Harbor, the small summer resort on Oregon's windswept coast. But the burning need to take some action to try and unlock the door to his past had easily outweighed their protests.

And while it was rewarding that the first person he met appeared to recognize him, his fervent hope that just such an occurrence might be the catalyst needed to jar his memory, quickly faded and died.

Frustration gave an edge to his voice. "How do you know me?" Dylan asked with some urgency, and watched in fascination as the expression in her soft brown eyes swiftly changed from startled joy to stark disbelief.

Maggie stared at Dylan in stunned silence. He was teasing her. He had to be! But she could see no glint of humor in his eyes, no welcoming smile, not even the faintest flicker of recognition.

"You don't remember me?" Maggie forced the words past lips that were trembling, fighting now to control the bubble of hysteria threatening to burst free.

Dylan's frown deepened, and Maggie held her breath as his gaze swept over her once more. But when his gray eyes returned to hers, all she could see was tension, anger and a deep frustration.

Even before he opened his mouth to reply she already knew his answer, and the pain suddenly slicing through her swiftly eradicated the feelings of joy that had erupted when she'd first heard his voice.

"No...I'm sorry. I don't remember you." Dylan spoke the words he'd been repeating more often than he cared to think about during the past four months.

But what choice did he have? He couldn't lie. And much as he might want to ease the anxiety he could see shimmering in the depths of the young woman's eyes...much as he wanted desperately to remember something...he didn't.

He didn't remember her. He didn't remember anything.

The doctors at the hospital in San Diego had told him he was lucky to be alive, that if his seat belt hadn't been securely fastened when the truck crossed the median and ran headlong into his car, he'd have been just another statistic.

He'd spent four months in a coma and awakened not knowing who he was or where he was. His memories, his past, his life, had all been erased.

It had taken another four months of intense therapy, both physical and mental, to restore some semblance of normalcy to his life, and while he'd made great progress and regained a good deal of his strength, his memories had remained locked inside him.

Not until he'd started cleaning out his quarters at the base had he come across the stack of mail that had accumulated since the accident. It was there he'd found the letters from a lawyer in Grace Harbor informing him he was a beneficiary in his aunt's and her husband's will.

The letters had been the catalyst that set him on the road to Grace Harbor. The moment he read them he decided to take control of his life and go in search of the key to unlock his past.

Dylan felt the young woman before him sway, bringing him back to the present. He tightened his hold and glanced at her pale features in time to see a look of pain darken her eyes.

"Are you all right? Is it the baby?" Dylan asked anxiously.

"No," came the shaky reply, in a voice scarcely more than a whisper.

"Maybe you should sit down," Dylan suggested, concern for the woman and her unborn child uppermost in his mind.

"No…really. I'm okay," Maggie insisted.

Taking a step back, Maggie broke free of Dylan's hold, all the while wondering if she'd somehow stumbled into a nightmare.

At that moment, as if to remind her of its existence, the baby began repeatedly to kick her. "Oh…" Maggie winced, and instinctively her hand moved to her stomach.

"Maybe you should see a doctor," Dylan said, convinced he was the cause of her distress. "Or I could call your husband."

"I'm not married," Maggie replied abruptly.

"Oh…then let me drive you home. My car is parked—"

"No! Please…it's not necessary," she cut in. "The baby's active, that's all," she explained, wondering for a fleeting second if the child had somehow sensed its father's presence.

As this thought registered, it was all Maggie could do to hold back the tears suddenly stinging her eyes. She dropped her gaze, silently admonishing herself for her weakness.

But her emotions these days seemed to be very close to the surface. This unexpected and strange encounter with Dylan was taking its toll, and she knew she was liable at any moment to burst into tears.

She swallowed the lump of emotion lodged in her throat. "I just came from the doctor's office," she explained. "I'm on my way home," she added, trying to keep the telltale tremor from her voice.

"Let me drive you," Dylan offered.

"It's not necessary," she quickly countered, wanting to be alone. Seeing Dylan again, a Dylan who gave no indication whatsoever that he even knew her, was having a profound effect on her.

There had been times throughout her pregnancy when she'd dreamed of his return, imagining a sweet and joyous reunion. But never in her wildest moments had she envisioned a scene quite like the one playing out now.

"Fine," Dylan responded easily. "But I insist on seeing you home safely," he said.

Maggie didn't have the energy to refuse. Bizarre as the situation was, and distraught as she felt by the fact that he didn't remember her, in a small corner of her heart she was still clinging to the hope that there was some reasonable explanation for Dylan's unusual behavior.

"All right. Thank you," Maggie relented.

"Good. Lean on me." Dylan offered her his arm.

Maggie's heart shuddered to a standstill. "I can manage," she told him, though her voice sounded husky. But she knew if she touched Dylan now, the thin thread of her control would surely snap in two.

It was as they silently made their slow ascent up Indigo Street that Maggie noticed Dylan was wearing a white T-shirt and a pair of old, faded, blue jeans.

Gone was the naval uniform she was accustomed to seeing, and gone too was the regulation haircut synonymous with men who served their country.

His jet-black hair now curled invitingly at the nape of his neck, and Maggie noted with some surprise that he appeared to have lost weight.

Had he been ill? she wondered.

"How far is it?" Dylan asked, cutting into her wayward thoughts.

Maggie darted him a questioning glance.

"At the crest of the hill," she told him, finding it more than a little strange having to relate this information.

Dylan knew exactly where she lived. He'd stayed at Fairwinds eight months ago—had spent the night making love to her, first with a frenzied passion that had thrilled and electrified her, and again with an aching tenderness that had touched her soul and moved her immeasurably.

Could he really have forgotten?

But what other explanation was there? Either he was a damned good actor, or he really didn't remember her.

Maybe this man wasn't Dylan after all, she silently reasoned. Maybe he was someone who only looked like Dylan. Everyone had a double somewhere, didn't they?

But even as these wild notions flitted through Maggie's head, she knew she was only fooling herself.

"This is it." Her breathing somewhat labored, she slowed to a halt at the entrance to the driveway leading to the old Georgian-style house Maggie ran as a bed-and-breakfast.

"Fairwinds." Dylan read the name painted in black and gold on the sign that faced the street. His gaze shifted to the large three-story structure nestled amid a stand of tall fir trees and several silver birches.

Maggie darted him a curious glance. Not only did Dylan not remember her, he didn't appear to remember Fairwinds. If that was the case, what had brought him to Grace Harbor?

While she longed to ask the question, Maggie wasn't altogether sure she wanted to hear the answer.

Digging in her purse, she located her keys. She stood for a moment, at a loss to know what to say or do. Should she invite him in? No…she really wasn't feeling up to dealing with this inexplicable situation. It was all so confusing.

"Thank you for walking me home," she said, before turning and heading down the driveway.

"Wait!" Dylan called out, and when her head whipped round to look at him, he caught the glimmer of hope that flashed in her eyes. "You didn't answer my question," he said.

"Question?" she repeated with a frown.

"How do you know me?" Dylan asked, and to his astonishment, watched as her eyes filled with tears. Startled, he took a step toward her. "I've upset you. I'm sorry. It wasn't my intention—"

"Please—I can't do this. I have to go..." Maggie spun away and hurried toward the house.

Dylan stood for a long moment watching her departing figure. She knew him, that much was certain, but her reaction baffled him.

Damn! He wished his memories weren't locked inside his head...wished— Gritting his teeth, he clamped down on his thoughts.

Wishing didn't accomplish anything; that much he'd learned. The doctors had told him to rely on his instincts, to listen to and trust his inner feelings. And right now they were shouting at him to follow the young woman.

Dylan strode down the driveway after her. Quickening his pace, he reached the front door just as she was preparing to close it.

Surprise and another emotion he couldn't decipher flashed in the depths of her brown eyes when she saw him.

"Look, I'm sorry if I've upset you, but I'd really like to talk to you...." He stopped to catch his breath, and as he inhaled he caught the sweet scent of the roses blooming in the planter under the front window.

Suddenly a chill raced through his body, and dizziness blurred his vision. Pain exploded inside his head, and like a soldier felled by a sniper's bullet, he sank to his knees as a kaleidoscope of lights flashed behind his eyes.

His heart was pounding, and he covered his eyes with his hands as the pain inside his head became so intense he thought he might black out.

"What's wrong? Are you ill?" The feminine voice filled with anxiety and concern came from somewhere nearby, but for the life of him Dylan couldn't respond.

"Can you get up?" the same voice asked, and he felt a pair of hands gently grasp his arm.

Dylan scrambled to his feet. His legs felt like two rubber bands, and he struggled to remain upright.

Fighting to stay calm, Maggie helped Dylan into the house. Something was horribly wrong.

"I'll call a doctor," she said as she led him into the spacious living room and urged him into the near- est armchair.

"No! No, doctors." Dylan's tone was emphatic. He'd seen enough doctors during the past four months to last him a lifetime. Besides, the throbbing in his head was beginning to subside.

With some relief he ventured to open his eyes and, glancing up, found himself staring into a pair of anx- ious brown eyes, eyes that for a fleeting second seemed familiar.

"What happened?" Maggie asked, fear and con- cern warring within her.

"To tell you the truth, I'm not exactly sure," Dylan responded as he ran a hand through his hair. A frown creased his features. "Nothing like that's ever hap- pened to me before," he told her. "Although the doc- tors did warn me about headaches…"

Maggie felt her heart leap in startled reaction. "Doctors?" She repeated.

Dylan nodded. "I was in a car accident a few months back," he explained.

"An accident?" Maggie felt the blood drain from her face. "What happened?" She pushed the question past a throat that was suddenly dry, and although she managed to sound calm, inside she was trembling like a leaf.

Dylan leaned forward, resting his elbows on his thighs. Clasping his hands together, he studied them for a long moment before answering. "A truck crossed the median and hit my car head-on," he told her in a voice devoid of emotion.

Maggie bit down on the inner softness of her mouth to stop the moan from escaping, as images of Dylan slumped over the wheel of his car, bleeding and unconscious, flashed into her mind.

A queasiness, reminiscent of the morning sickness that had attacked her during the early part of her pregnancy, washed over her. Her legs threatened to give way, and she quickly lowered herself into the armchair opposite him.

"How...how badly were you hurt?" Maggie asked, and saw his whole body tense at her question.

Her gaze shifted to his hands clasped tightly together, their knuckles already turning white.

"I suffered trauma to the head, a broken collarbone, lacerations, a broken leg and various minor cuts and bruises," he said, reeling off the list of injuries as if he was reading a grocery list.

Maggie sucked in a startled breath and felt her stomach heave.

Dylan heard the soft gasp and, glancing at the young woman, noted the paleness of her features.

With a muttered curse he rose from the chair and knelt in front of her.

"I'm sorry. Forgive me. I don't know what I was thinking," he said, genuine regret in his tone. "But you're the first person to come right out and ask me that question."

Maggie smiled weakly, while her heart stumbled against her ribs in reaction to his nearness.

"I'd better go," Dylan said, rising to his feet. "I seem to be making a habit of upsetting you. No...don't get up," he hurried on. "I'll see myself out."

Turning, he headed toward the door, but he hadn't taken more than three steps, when he saw the beautiful antique mahogany bureau to the left of the doorway. A brass-framed photograph sat on its highly polished surface, and when his gaze fell on the two people in the picture, he came to an abrupt halt.

His heart shuddered to a standstill when he realized that the photograph was identical to the one he'd found on his desk in his living quarters at the base.

Snatching the frame from off the bureau, he spun around.

"How do you know these people? Why do you have this photograph?" Dylan fired the questions at her.

Maggie's pulse took a crazy leap at the intense expression on Dylan's face. She couldn't for the life of her understand his strange reaction.

Dylan had been there the day the picture had been taken, that sunny afternoon in June, five years ago when his Aunt Rosemary had married her father, William Fairchild.

Maggie doubted she would ever forget that day. It

was the first time she'd set eyes on Dylan. He'd driven all the way from San Diego just to give his aunt away, and Maggie could still recall how incredibly handsome he'd looked walking down the aisle wearing the dress uniform of a lieutenant commander in the United States Navy.

"Tell me!" Dylan demanded as he retraced his steps.

Maggie could feel the tension coming off him in waves. Meeting his gaze, she saw a look of anguish in the steel gray depths of his eyes.

A shiver danced down her spine. What on earth was going on? Why was Dylan so agitated, so frantic?

"The man in the picture is my father," she told him.

"Your father? My aunt married your father?" Dylan's expression was incredulous.

"Yes," Maggie replied. Why was he asking these questions when he already knew the answer? Confusion and anger stirred to life within her. "I don't understand what's going on here," she said. "You were there at the wedding. You gave your aunt away. Don't you remember?"

Dylan's gaze flicked back to the photograph he held in his hand. Not for the first time since coming out of the accident-induced coma, he silently willed himself to remember.

"No! Dammit! I don't remember," he enunciated every word carefully, his voice reverberating with barely suppressed anger.

"You don't remember your aunt's wedding?" Maggie repeated, confused by his response.

Dylan's eyes snapped to meet hers. "That's right...I don't remember my aunt's wedding," he parroted, exasperation and despair echoing through his words.

And suddenly Maggie understood. "The accident...all those injuries...you've lost your memory." It was the only explanation that made any sense.

"That's right," Dylan confirmed, his tone grim.

"But, surely—" Maggie began, still having trouble grasping the situation.

"Wait! If my aunt married your father," he jumped in, "then it stands to reason you were at the wedding, too." Retracing his steps he set the photograph back on the bureau.

"Yes, I was there," Maggie said.

He turned to face her. "So, we were all friends— your father and my aunt, you and me...we'd all known each other for a while?" he asked, an eagerness in his tone that puzzled Maggie.

"Not quite," she replied, and saw the flash of disappointment in his eyes. "That was the first time I...that we'd met," she told him, refraining from adding that the meeting had changed her life.

"I see," he said on a sigh. "I was hoping...I thought maybe..." He ground to a halt. "Do you have any idea how terrifying it is to wake up and not know who you are?" he suddenly asked.

Maggie heard the fear and helplessness in Dylan's voice, and her heart went out to him. But before she could say anything, he spoke again.

"I lay staring at the ceiling trying to remember my name. I mean...everyone knows their own name, right?" he appealed to her, and she nodded.

"But my mind was a complete blank," he said. "I had no idea who I was, no idea what the doctors were asking me or telling me.

"They told me my memory would probably come back in a day or two...but after two weeks I still couldn't remember anything. Eventually they told me my name and that I was a naval officer, in the hope it would help me remember. It didn't...nothing did."

He lapsed into silence, and Maggie held her breath waiting for him to continue.

"Weeks went by and I began to wonder if I had a family, if there was anyone who might be able to tell me more about my past, my life." Dylan went on. "I asked the nurses if anyone had visited me while I was in a coma. When they scurried off to get the doctor I knew something was wrong...."

"What did they tell you?" Maggie asked, her head still buzzing from the knowledge that he'd been in a coma. She was beginning, in a very small way, to get a sense of how devastated and disoriented Dylan must have felt at the realization he had no identity.

"They told me—" his voice cracked "—they told me I had an aunt, who according to my records, was the only relative...the only family I had."

Maggie's heart skipped a beat. "But, she's—" She stopped abruptly when his gray eyes darted to meet hers.

"Dead?" Dylan finished for her.

Maggie nodded. "So you do remember something," she began tentatively, only to lapse into silence when his jaw tightened and a look of despair turned his eyes a dismal gray.

"I remember nothing," Dylan corrected, his body quivering with renewed anger.

She stared at him for a long moment as the enormity of what he was saying began to sink in. "You mean you don't remember that your aunt and my father died in a plane crash. You don't remember coming here for their funeral. You don't remember—'' Maggie broke off, her tone hollow with despair.

"I don't remember one single, solitary thing about any event in my past.... Nothing!'' Dylan clamped down on the anger spiraling through him, annoyed with himself for indulging in a display of such blatant self-pity.

"But...the doctors... Did they say if you'll ever get it back?'' Maggie stumbled over the question.

Dylan sank into the chair he'd vacated a short time ago and gazed across at her, his expression unreadable. "Unfortunately none of the doctors or specialists I was paraded in front of would give me a straight answer on that one.''

"You mean you may never get your memory back?'' she asked incredulously.

Dylan's sigh was long and loud. "Amnesia is a condition that varies from person to person depending on the circumstances and the degree of trauma that brought it on,'' he recited, almost as if he was reading the words directly from a medical textbook. "There's no guarantee it will return. There's no guarantee it won't.''

Maggie heard the torment in his voice, glimpsed the anguish in his eyes, and the urge to reach out and offer comfort almost swamped her.

"I'm so sorry,'' she said, but Dylan didn't seem to hear.

"You know, it's strange,'' Dylan said, a sad smile on his face, "but the worst thing about all this isn't that I've lost my memory, though believe me, that's been terrifying enough. It was finding out I have no family, no one who could help me fill in my past, no one who can help me piece together who I really am.

"Aunt Rosemary was my only relative...and she's gone. I'm completely and utterly alone in the world—" He broke off, dropping his head onto his hands in a gesture that tore at Maggie's heart.

"That's not true. You do have family," she blurted out, unable to stay silent.

Dylan's head jerked up, and he looked at her in astonishment.

"What do you mean?" he asked, his gaze holding her captive.

Maggie drew a steadying breath. "You're not alone. You do have family," she said.

Dylan frowned. "I don't understand."

Maggie put her hand on her abdomen in a protective gesture. "This baby...the baby I'm carrying, is yours...."

Chapter Two

The moment the words were out Maggie regretted them. Dylan's jaw dropped open, and he stared at her as if she'd suddenly sprouted horns.

"Are you serious?" Dylan asked in disbelief, and for the second time in as many minutes, Maggie wished she hadn't spoken.

But as she'd listened to Dylan talk about having no family, of being alone in the world, she'd simply responded to his soulful cry without a thought to the consequences.

Biting back a sigh, Maggie felt the undulating movement as the baby shifted positions, gently prodding her low in her abdomen.

"I'm serious," she assured him softly. Easing herself out of the chair, she crossed to the window, all the while gently massaging the area where she could feel one tiny foot or elbow poking her.

"But how?" With a perplexed look Dylan sank back against the upholstery.

Maggie glanced at him, and seeing the expression on his handsome face, knew he had doubts about her declaration. She couldn't really blame him. "I'm sorry," she said. "You obviously have enough to contend with at the moment."

Dylan studied his hands for a time. "I...well...it is quite a shock," he said at last. "Uh...when is the baby due?"

"June twenty-second," she responded. "At least that's what my doctor tells me." She started to walk the length of the room to where a stone fireplace filled the far wall.

Dylan followed her progress, slowly surveying the rounded contours of her body, from the fullness of her breasts to the voluptuous mound of fertility beneath the pink and white cotton maternity dress she wore.

There was something innately beautiful, as well as indefinably sensual, about a woman carrying a child...any child. But if he was to believe her...this child was his.

He drew a shaky breath and felt his heart shudder inside his chest as the enormity of the situation gripped him.

But surely he wouldn't have forgotten making love with her? Or forgotten how her body felt beneath his, their mouths fused, their limbs entwined in passion, a passion that had resulted in the creation of another human being.

Dylan squeezed his eyes tight and willed himself to remember. But there was nothing, only a black empty void that was his past, that was his life.

But he couldn't, in good conscience, ignore or dismiss what she'd just told him, and there had been an unmistakable ring of truth in her voice.

Suddenly Dylan recalled the warmth he'd seen in her eyes when they'd collided in the street, a warmth quickly replaced with a look of pain and wariness.

But if what she said was true, if he was the father of her child, then it was both reasonable and logical to assume a relationship had existed between them prior to his accident.

After his recent release from the hospital, he'd returned to his quarters at the base, but he'd found nothing that would indicate any such relationship existed.

Something was definitely amiss.

Dylan sighed and covered his face with his hands. The puzzle that was his past had taken a new and astonishing twist.

Gut instinct, combined with the letters he had found in his desk had brought him to Grace Harbor. Following through on his instincts had already paid off. He'd only been in town a few hours and he'd already made several new discoveries, but none more remarkable than her stunning declaration.

"You really don't remember...anything?" Her voice cut into the lengthy silence.

The hint of a smile tugged at his mouth as Dylan shook his head. "I wish I did," he said, and Maggie heard the frustration in his voice.

She watched as he rose from the chair and paced the length of the room.

"What's strange about all this," Dylan said, ignoring the pain in his left leg, "is that when I awoke from the coma I knew how to do simple, everyday tasks, all the things a person learns throughout the natural process of growing up.

"It's the personal memories, anything that would reveal something about my past, about relationships in my life, about who I am…all that has been wiped out." He came to a halt in front of her.

"I feel lost…as if I've been cast out into the sea without a life preserver, and I'm struggling to keep my head above the water."

The pain vibrating through his voice tore at Maggie's heart, and not for the first time she felt the urge to reach out and offer comfort.

"It must be very difficult for you," she said, keeping her tone even. "I wish there was something I could do."

Dylan's sigh was heartfelt. "I don't remember you…or your name—and you're telling me you're having my baby—" He broke off, and Maggie caught the ripple of movement at his throat as he swallowed convulsively. "I defy anyone not to feel a little overwhelmed," he challenged.

Maggie met his silver gaze and suddenly the air between them crackled with tension. Every nerve in her body throbbed with anticipation, crying out to feel his arms around her, to experience again the magic of his mouth on hers.

"What *is* your name?" Dylan asked, effectively breaking the spell.

"Maggie," she told him huskily. "Maggie Fairchild."

"Maggie. Maggie," he repeated softly, closing his eyes.

The sound of her name on his lips was like a lover's tender caress, and a shudder of longing sprinted through her. She held her breath and sent up a silent prayer for herself and her unborn baby.

"I'm sorry. I don't remember." Dylan's words squashed the tiny seed of hope lingering in her heart, and when she looked into his eyes once more, it was to see both sorrow and despair in their stormy depths.

"But…if you really don't remember anything, why did you come to Grace Harbor?" Maggie asked.

"Because it was the first and only link I had to my past," Dylan replied.

"I don't understand."

"Two weeks ago, after I was released from the hospital, I was going through a pile of mail, mail that had accumulated in my quarters since the accident," he explained.

"Among the flyers and junk mail were two letters from a lawyer here in Grace Harbor…his name is Jared something." He frowned and fumbled in the pocket of his jeans for the letters.

"McAndrew," Maggie supplied.

"That's right." Dylan abandoned his search. "In the first letter he mentioned he was the executor for the estate of Rosemary and William Fairchild, and I was a beneficiary and would I please contact him as soon as possible. The second letter was a repeat of the first."

Dylan glanced at Maggie. "You must be a beneficiary, too."

"Yes, I am," Maggie replied.

"Then you know the contents of the will," he said.

"Yes," she acknowledged. "But I think you should talk to Jared," she said in a hurry, seeing the questions in his eyes.

"I was on my way to his office when I bumped into you," Dylan told her. "I suppose it's too late now, to drop in on him."

A wave of tiredness washed over Maggie. She glanced at the clock on the oak mantelpiece above the fireplace noting it was only a little past five.

She felt physically as well as emotionally drained. During her checkup earlier, Dr. Whitney had asked how well she was sleeping, and she'd reported that of late she'd suffered a few sleepless nights. The doctor had recommended she rest or take a nap whenever the need arose, and the urge to do just that was on her now.

"Actually, it isn't too late," Maggie heard herself say. "Jared has a reputation around town for being something of a workaholic. I'm sure he'll still be in his office."

Dylan noted the look of weariness in Maggie's eyes and realized that their encounter had taken its toll on her, too.

"I'll head there now and see if I can catch him," Dylan said. "But, there's still a lot we have to...ah...discuss. Perhaps I can come back tomorrow?"

"I'm not going anywhere," Maggie said, feeling sure he'd be back right after he talked to Jared.

Dylan withdrew, and when she heard the front door close behind him, Maggie crossed to the window, watching until he was out of sight.

Beneath her heart the baby began a series of kicks, as if trying to attract her attention. Maggie smiled, and with a circling motion she began to massage her abdomen as she made her way from the living room.

As she was wont to do these days, she headed straight for the baby's room where a few months ago, using paint and a box of decals depicting jungle animals, she'd transformed the small bedroom into a bright and colorful nursery.

She'd bought a changing table with a bath, as well as a dresser that she'd already half filled with tiny sleepers and blankets and a variety of necessary items.

She'd unearthed the old rocking chair her father had stored in the garage, and she'd stripped it and refinished it herself. Now it sat on the oval rug that covered the polished hardwood floor.

All that was missing was the crib, which had been delivered a few days ago and was leaning against the wall, still unassembled.

Maggie lowered herself into the rocker, and gazed up at the mobile of jungle animals she'd suspended from the light fixture. The soft summer breeze drifting in through the open window made the animals dance.

Reaching over, she pulled open a dresser drawer. Her fingers closed around a tiny knitted sweater. Her mother had died when Maggie was five, but her father had often spoken about his wife's talent for knitting.

Maggie had rummaged through some old boxes in the garage and unearthed some of her mother's old knitting patterns. She'd bought wool at the local craft store and with a little help from the woman who ran the store, Maggie had followed a simple pattern and knitted a plain white shawl as well as several baby sweaters.

As Maggie hugged the tiny sweater, her thoughts shifted to those moments when she'd told Dylan he was the baby's father. She doubted she'd ever forget the look of disbelief on his face or the way his eyes had turned a steely gray.

Seven months ago when Dr. Whitney had told her the nausea and sickness she'd been experiencing wasn't a bout of flu after all, she'd reacted in much the same way.

Her initial shock had quickly evaporated, replaced by a feeling of intense and irrepressible joy. Learning that the night she'd spent with Dylan had resulted in his seed being planted in her womb, had only confirmed in her heart that what they'd shared had indeed been incredibly special.

Believing he had a right to know, her first instinct had been to call the naval base in San Diego and tell him about the baby. But recalling Dylan's parting words about not believing in love, after that incredible night of making love, she'd changed her mind.

When she'd learned the contents of her father's and Rosemary's will, her hopes had risen again, feeling sure Dylan would return to claim his inheritance.

But five months later, when her pregnancy was no longer a secret and had become the source of gossip in town, Dylan had not responded to Jared's letters, and the doubts and fears had started to crowd in.

Now Dylan was back, but he wasn't the same man who'd stolen her heart so long ago. He was a stranger.

When Dylan reached the foot of Indigo Street and made the turn onto Grace Harbor's main thoroughfare, he extracted the lawyer's letter from the back pocket of his jeans.

Checking the address, he noted that Jared McAndrew's law office was less than three blocks away.

As he walked along the sidewalk, he found his thoughts drifting back to Maggie and her startling announcement.

Was she telling the truth? Had they been lovers? Was the child she carried really his?

Suddenly Dylan felt his heart begin to race as a feeling of panic, not unlike the emotions he'd experienced after waking up from the coma, assailed him.

He slowed to a halt and leaned on a nearby lamppost waiting for his heart rate to return to normal, wondering if the idea of becoming a father, of being responsible for the care and welfare of a baby had caused his sudden and strange reaction.

The fact that he had no memories of his own childhood, or of his own father, and knew nothing about parenting was no doubt an added factor.

From what little he'd been able to piece together, he'd been fostered out to several families during his early life. It hadn't been until he was a teenager that his aunt had taken him under her wing. He'd lived with her for several years before enlisting.

Dylan drew a steadying breath and continued on his way. He crossed the intersection and, after reaching the opposite curb, a quick glance at the numbers on the brass plaque on the brick face of the building on his right confirmed he'd found Jared McAndrew's office.

He stood for a moment enjoying the tangy smell of the ocean as it wafted to him on the soft breeze and mingled with the faint scent of the flowers hanging from baskets on the street lamps.

Before leaving San Diego, he'd paid a visit to one of the therapists who'd been helping him cope with the trauma of losing his memory.

Simon Bradford had been the only doctor who'd encouraged him to make the trip to Grace Harbor, suggesting Dylan might be fortunate enough to experience a situation that would stimulate his senses, evoking a response that would breach the barrier his subconscious mind had erected.

Suddenly Dylan's thoughts shifted to those moments when he'd dropped to his knees on the front step of Maggie's house, recalling once again the fragmented images that had flashed in his mind.

The pain in his head had been so intense he'd forgotten all about the images, and now his instincts were telling him that his subconscious had been reacting to something—what, he wasn't exactly sure—but something had definitely triggered his reaction…a memory perhaps?

A feeling of excitement surged through Dylan, and for the first time since waking from the coma he felt his spirits rise.

With a new eagerness he reached for the brass door handle and entered the offices of Jared McAndrew, Attorney at Law.

Inside, an old oak counter polished to a rich shine brought him to a halt. Behind the counter, nestled near the window, stood a beautiful antique desk complete with a leather desk set, a telephone and two wooden filing trays each overflowing with papers.

The wall at the rear of the office was one enormous bookcase, and a rich smell of wood polish, mingling with the scent of old books and fine leather, permeated the room.

"I thought I heard the door. May I help you?" A man in his mid- to late thirties, dressed in gray slacks, a matching gray silk vest atop a pristine white shirt unbuttoned at the collar, appeared out of the blue and approached the counter.

"I certainly hope so," Dylan responded. "My name is Dylan O'Connor. I received—"

"Mr. O'Connor! This is a surprise," the man interjected. "Please, come through," he invited as he deftly lifted a section of the polished wood counter.

"I'm Jared McAndrew," he said, extending his hand in welcome when Dylan joined him. "It's a pleasure to meet you."

Jared McAndrew's smile was friendly, his handshake firm and strong. "When you didn't acknowledge my last letter, I was seriously contemplating hiring a private detective to track you down."

"I'm here now," Dylan replied, offering no explanation for not responding to the letters.

The lawyer held Dylan's gaze for a long moment as if sizing him up. "Let's go into my office," Jared said, pointing to the open door on his left. "Please go right on in. I'll just lock the front door, that way we won't be disturbed."

Dylan did as he was bid. Jared McAndrew's office was relatively small but it, too, contained a beautiful oak desk, piled high with open files and large law books.

"Won't you sit down," Jared McAndrew invited when he reappeared. "I actually have your file right here." He lifted a bundle of papers and rummaged beneath them. "I was looking at it this morning," he added. "Ah...here it is."

Dylan said nothing. He leaned back in the comfortable leather chair across from Jared and waited for the lawyer to continue.

"I had the pleasure of meeting your aunt on several occasions, Mr. O'Connor," Jared said. "She was a lovely woman. Belated as they are, please accept my condolences on your loss."

"Thank you," Dylan responded evenly.

"Bill—ah...that is Mr. Fairchild and your aunt de-
rived a great deal of pleasure from the trips they took
together," Jared continued as he cleared a space on
his desk.

Dylan smiled and nodded.

"Hmm...well, Mr. O'Connor. You and Maggie,
that is Ms. Margaret Mary Fairchild are joint beneficiaries of the estate of the late Mr. and Mrs. William
Fairchild.

"There were a number of small bequests," he went
on as he surveyed the document before him. "As executor of the estate I've already taken care of those."

Dylan watched as Jared McAndrew leaned back in
his chair and steepled his fingers. "I can read you all
the legal jargon, but the long and the short of it, Mr.
O'Connor, is that as a joint beneficiary of the estate
of William and Rosemary Fairchild, you now own
half of the house and business known as Fairwinds,
situated at the address on Indigo Street in Grace
Harbor."

"Did you say business?" Dylan asked, frowning
now.

"That's right," Jared replied. "Fairwinds is a bed-
and-breakfast inn."

"Really?" Dylan said, surprise evident in his
voice. The sign outside the house had simply read
"Fairwinds" nothing more, and he was almost sure
he and Maggie had been alone in the big old house.

Jared McAndrew threw Dylan a puzzled look.
"Maggie has been running Fairwinds as a bed-and-
breakfast for the past five years," he explained. "It's
usually open from early spring through to late fall,"
the lawyer continued. "But this year...well, she's

postponed the opening, because she's having a baby."

"I see," Dylan commented.

"Have you talked to Maggie?" Jared McAndrew asked.

"Only briefly," Dylan replied, trying with difficulty to absorb all the lawyer had said.

"Then you'll know she has some strong ideas about Fairwinds," Jared McAndrew commented.

"Actually, we didn't discuss it," Dylan replied.

Jared McAndrew leaned forward to rest his forearms on the desk. "My advice is to sell and split the proceeds, but Maggie refuses to even consider it. She wants to go ahead and hire someone to take care of general maintenance and repairs."

"Maintenance and repairs?" Dylan repeated, feeling a little lost.

"Fairwinds is in dire need of a new roof, and the back stairs leading to the porch are hazardous and should be replaced," Jared informed him.

"I see," Dylan said.

"It's only my opinion, mind you," the lawyer continued, "but I think running a bed-and-breakfast is too much for her on her own, what with the baby due in a few weeks."

"Doesn't she have anyone working for her?" Dylan asked.

"She hires a student during the summer, but not this year," Jared explained. "I know Fairwinds is a popular place with tourists, but those repairs need to be undertaken for fear of accidents and subsequent lawsuits. Unless, of course, you're willing to do the work yourself. Are you handy with a hammer, Mr. O'Connor?"

"I really don't—" Dylan ground to a halt. In truth he didn't know whether or not he was capable of doing the work Jared McAndrew had described.

"You probably don't have the time," Jared went on easily. "I'm assuming you're here on leave."

"In a fashion," Dylan said, without elaborating.

"Then I suggest you discuss the matter of what to do with Fairwinds with Maggie as soon as possible," Jared advised.

"Oh...never fear, Mr. McAndrew, I intend to do just that," Dylan replied.

Chapter Three

Half an hour later Dylan retraced his steps along Grace Harbor's main street, wondering why Maggie hadn't mentioned they were joint beneficiaries.

On reaching his car, he unlocked the door and, stifling a groan, slid behind the wheel.

His left leg had taken a beating in the accident, a nasty break by all accounts. All in all his entire body had suffered. And while intense physical therapy and an exercise regime had helped restore a good portion of his mobility and flexibility, he knew he'd never again be one hundred percent fit.

That was what had prompted his decision to resign his commission, a decision his superiors had, at first, refused to accept, suggesting he simply take a long leave of absence, assuring him that once his memory returned, he'd be welcomed back without question.

But Dylan had been adamant, determined to listen to his gut instincts, which were telling him that even if his memory returned, his reduced level of fitness would prevent him from returning to active duty, and he'd sensed he wasn't the kind of man who'd enjoy sitting behind a desk shuffling papers.

Pulling out of the parking space, Dylan headed up Indigo Street. As he made the turn into Fairwinds, he drove the car directly to the rear of the house, bringing it to a halt in front of a freestanding garage and workshop.

Dylan shut off the motor and suddenly a wave of nausea washed over him. Leaning forward, he closed his eyes and lowered his head onto the steering wheel. He could feel the beads of perspiration forming on his forehead and hear his heart thundering inside his chest.

Inhaling deeply, he raised his head and opened his eyes. His gaze came to rest on the painted door of the garage, and all at once a clear image flashed into his mind.

He knew with a startling certainty that if he looked behind the closed garage door, he'd find a beautifully restored black, Model T Ford.

Dylan climbed from the car, and on legs that were shaky he went to the garage door. His head was beginning to throb, but the need to find out if he was right, to know if he'd actually remembered something, spurred him on.

Bending over, he curled his fingers around the handle, and twisting it, he began to lift the garage door. He took a step back as the door creaked and groaned on its metal track.

When the front bumper of a car came into view, the bitter taste of disappointment filled Dylan's mouth and he stumbled against the doorway. The vehicle parked in the garage was a blue four-door compact station wagon.

In the kitchen Maggie heard the familiar grinding noise of the garage door. Grabbing the portable telephone in case she needed to call the police to report a break-in, she hurried through the open French doors leading onto the porch.

The sight of Dylan leaning against the doorway of the garage sent her pulse racing.

"Is anything wrong?" Maggie called out.

Dylan spun around, and for a fleeting moment Maggie thought he looked on the verge of collapse.

"No," he replied before making his way toward the stairs leading up to the porch. "Did your father ever own an antique car?" he asked as he reached the top step.

Maggie heard the tension in his voice and noted, too, the taut line of his jaw as he waited for her answer.

"Ah…yes, he had—"

"An old Model T," Dylan quickly cut in.

"That's right," Maggie said.

"I knew it," Dylan said triumphantly.

"My father loved to tinker with old cars," she went on. "He restored the Model T himself. It was his pride and…" Maggie stopped, suddenly realizing the significance of what had just happened. "You remembered something!" she said, and watched as his handsome features broke into a jubilant smile.

"Yes! I remembered something! I actually remembered something!" Dylan's joy was catching, and Maggie felt her heart leap into her throat at the excitement she could see in his eyes.

"That's wonderful," she heard herself say.

Dylan's expression sobered a little. "Without thinking I drove the car around to the back of the house. My guess is I've probably parked there before." He stopped and met Maggie's gaze, looking for confirmation.

"Yes, you have," she answered.

"I experienced the same sensation I felt outside earlier. But this time...well, I saw a clear picture in my mind, a picture of an old car. That's why I opened the garage door," Dylan explained. "What happened to the Model T?"

"My father sold it to a collector just before—" She faltered, a sadness engulfing her.

"Just before what?" Dylan asked, his brow creasing into a frown.

Blinking back tears, Maggie looked deeply into Dylan's gray eyes still finding it hard to believe he'd forgotten about the crash of the small plane that had killed her father and his aunt. "Just before they left on what was their last trip," she told him.

"Oh...I'm sorry." Dylan's hands came up to clasp her shoulders, and she gasped at the contact that sent a quiver of longing through her. "I didn't mean to upset you," he went on softly. "It's so damned frustrating. I just want my life back! I want all the empty spaces filled. I want to remember—" Dylan drew a ragged breath and dropped his hands to his sides.

"I understand...really," Maggie said. "Maybe you're just trying too hard," she added, his disappointment and frustration ringing in her ears. "Besides...you did remember something. You remembered the old Model T," she said. "It's a start."

Maggie watched as Dylan's mouth curved into the

ghost of a smile and felt her heart stumble against her rib cage in reaction.

"You're absolutely right," he said. "There's definitely something about this place," he added with a sigh. "By the way, why didn't you tell me we were joint owners?"

Maggie swallowed and dropped her gaze. "I thought it would be best, in the circumstances, if Jared told you."

"I see," Dylan said. "Your lawyer friend also mentioned that you run…ah…Fairwinds as a bed-and-breakfast, but that you haven't opened for business this season because of the baby."

"That's right," Maggie replied. "Let's talk about this inside, shall we? Dinner is almost ready."

Dylan threw her a startled glance.

Maggie turned and headed toward the open kitchen door. "I felt sure once Jared told you we were joint owners you'd be back," she said, a faint edge to her tone.

Setting the phone back on the counter, Maggie moved to the sink where she'd been cutting up tomatoes and mushrooms and rinsing romaine lettuce to make a salad.

"How many rooms does Fairwinds have?" Dylan asked, closing the French doors behind him.

"Six," Maggie said. "Four have their own bathrooms," she added as she broke off a leaf from the lettuce sitting on a towel on the drain-board.

"McAndrew mentioned something about the house needing a few repairs," Dylan commented, crossing to the kitchen table where two places had already been set.

"Jared's right," Maggie acknowledged. "My father usually took care of the general maintenance, but after he and Rosemary were married they were always flying off on some adventure, and things started to deteriorate. Now Fairwinds needs a few repairs. I'm sure Jared told you his recommendation.'' She glanced over her shoulder as she tore the lettuce leaf into bite-size pieces.

"To put Fairwinds on the market, you mean?'' Dylan pulled out a chair and sat down. "Yes, he did mention it. He also thinks we'll get a decent price because of its reputation and popularity with tourists. Is that true?''

"About its reputation? Yes,'' Maggie said with a mixture of pride and anger in her voice. She'd worked hard to put Fairwinds on the map, and she hated to have Jared, or anyone for that matter, regard it solely from a money-making perspective.

The house itself had been in her family for several generations, and with her father's approval and help, she'd turned it into a popular bed-and-breakfast. So far, the money she'd made each season had paid expenses and seen her through the winter. But during the past few years several problems have cropped up, and repairs needed to be done.

"I've had to turn away a few regular customers this season and reschedule others,'' she went on. "But, I plan to reopen Fairwinds the last weekend in July.''

She'd struggled with the decision about whether or not to hire someone to run the bed-and-breakfast for two months. But ultimately she'd decided Fairwinds's reputation for great food and first-class accommodation might be damaged if she handed the reins over to someone else.

Dr. Whitney had advised her to avoid any stress during the last month of her pregnancy. Closing Fairwinds for two months had seemed the best solution, and during that time she'd planned to hire someone to do the necessary repairs.

"McAndrew's suggestion that we put Fairwinds up for sale seems like the best solution," Dylan said.

Maggie flung the handful of greens into the bowl and turned to glare at Dylan.

"I will never agree to sell Fairwinds," Maggie stated, anger in every syllable. "This house was built by my great-grandfather and passed down to my grandfather, my father and now—" She broke off abruptly. "If it's money you want, I'll take out another mortgage and scrape up every penny I can to buy you out. But I refuse to put the house up for sale."

Dylan saw the flash of resentment in the depths of her calm brown eyes, and he recognized, too, the frustration in the tight line of her mouth and the edginess of her voice.

He raised his hands in mock surrender. "Forgive me. I had no idea Fairwinds had so much history…or that it means so much to you."

He hadn't really given much thought to being a joint owner of Fairwinds, he'd simply taken the lawyer's recommendation at face value.

"I just don't understand—" Maggie ground to a halt once more and returned to the task of making a salad.

"Why they made us joint beneficiaries?" Dylan said, filling in the blank.

Maggie froze for a moment, then deliberately tore the remaining lettuce leaf into small pieces before adding them to the bowl. Wiping her hands on the tea towel, she turned to look at him.

"Yes," she replied, unable to lie.

"I wish I knew the answer to that myself," said Dylan. He was silent for a moment. "Why don't you tell me about them?" he asked softly.

"Excuse me?" Maggie carried the bowl of salad to the table.

"Tell me about your father and my aunt," he said. "How did they meet?"

"They met on a cruise to Alaska," Maggie said, before turning to the stove. Pulling on a pair of oven gloves, she opened the oven door.

"Hold on! Let me do that." Dylan pushed back his chair and rose to his feet. Before Maggie had time to protest, he had relieved her of the gloves and put them on.

He carried a steaming chicken casserole to the table. "Hmm…this smells incredible," he said, inhaling the appetizing aroma of herbs and spices.

"Thank you," Maggie mumbled and, feeling her face grow warm at his comment, went to the fridge. "Would you like a glass of milk?"

"Yes, please," Dylan replied politely.

Maggie filled two glasses and set them on the table. Once seated, she served the moist and juicy chicken breasts cooked in a rich creamy mushroom sauce, and for several minutes they ate in companionable silence.

"This is delicious." Dylan flashed her a smile as he helped himself to a second piece of chicken.

"Thank you," Maggie said. "The recipe is one your aunt gave me," she told him.

"Really," Dylan replied. "You said they met on a cruise," he prompted.

"Yes. My father had just retired—"

"From what?"

Maggie set her fork and knife down. "He was a lawyer. The only one in town until Jared moved to Grace Harbor. He and my father teamed up for a year, then my father retired and Jared took over the law practice," she explained.

"I see," Dylan commented.

"My father had always wanted to take a cruise to Alaska," Maggie went on. "I bought him the ticket as a retirement present. Your aunt Rosemary won her trip, and according to her, she hadn't been too keen on going, at least not on her own." Maggie reached for the glass of milk, taking a sip before continuing.

"They were assigned the same table for their meals, and my father said seeing Rosemary every day was the highlight of his trip." Maggie smiled at the memory of how much in love her father had been and how fearful he'd been that she, his beloved daughter, wouldn't like or approve of his choice.

But Rosemary had been easy to like, a warm and generous woman, and clearly as in love with her father as he was with her. "They were married six months later."

"Are there any other wedding photographs?" Dylan asked. "I only found one, the same one you have."

"It was a very small wedding," Maggie said, still finding it strange having to relate to Dylan information he already knew. After all, he'd given his aunt away...albeit reluctantly. "I took a roll of pictures and Rosemary picked her favorites and had a few enlargements done. She put the rest in an album," Maggie said. "Would you like to see it?"

"Very much," he replied. "I'll clear away the dishes," he said.

"You don't have to—" Maggie began, but Dylan shook his head.

"It's the least I can do," he countered as he came around the table toward her. "Besides, I haven't forgotten how to wash and dry dishes, or load a dishwasher," he told her. "Oh...by the way, which is it?" He flashed a teasing grin.

Maggie's heart lurched in response to his grin, so uncharacteristic of the Dylan she remembered. "Dishwasher," she said. "It's to the right of the sink."

As she eased herself from the kitchen chair, Maggie felt the baby begin to kick wildly, and she let out a soft hiss of protest as she steadied herself against the table.

"Are you all right?" Dylan asked, his tone anxious.

Maggie glanced up to find Dylan staring directly at her abdomen, at the exact spot where she could feel the baby's fist or foot poking at her, causing her white cotton maternity dress to move.

"Is that—?" Dylan stopped and darted a quick startled look at her. "I'm sorry...it's just...well, I don't think I've ever...I mean..." He stumbled to a halt.

Maggie had to stifle the bubble of laughter threatening to surface. She doubted she'd ever seen such a bewildered expression on anyone's face before.

"Yes...that's the baby," Maggie confirmed. "He always gets active like this right after I've eaten. I think it's his way of saying thanks for his supper," she added with a smile.

"He?" Dylan's gaze shot to meet hers. "The baby's a boy?"

"Ah, no. At least, I don't know." Maggie quickly confessed, aware of the blush creeping up her neck and into her cheeks. "Sometimes when it's so active, kicking like a soccer player, I think it must be a boy. Other times, when the movements seem gentler, less aggressive. I think it's a girl," she said.

"Do they hurt? The kicks, I mean," Dylan asked, darting another fascinated glance at her abdomen.

"No," she assured him with a smile. "It's a strange sensation, but rather wonderful, though uncomfortable at times."

"I'd say it's pretty amazing," Dylan commented, and the quiet awe in his voice touched Maggie's heart.

Other than his initial stunned reaction to her announcement that the baby was his, Dylan had avoided the issue of her pregnancy, and in all honesty she couldn't really blame him.

But the look she could see in the depths of his eyes now held a mixture of curiosity, bewilderment and wonder. Without stopping to think, Maggie reached out to capture Dylan's wrist.

Meeting no resistance, she placed his hand near the area where the baby's foot was again nudging insistently at her.

When Dylan felt the brief but unmistakable jab beneath his fingers, his heart slammed against his chest and instinctively he jerked his hand away.

His gaze flew to meet Maggie's in time to see the flash of pain and disappointment that darkened her brown eyes. "I'm sorry," he heard himself say. "I didn't expect...I was startled, that's all," he went on. "Ah...may I?"

Maggie nodded, blinking back the tears stinging her eyes.

Dylan placed his hand on Maggie's abdomen once again, but this time he felt nothing but the texture of her maternity dress.

Disappointed, he started to withdraw but Maggie's hand quickly covered his and a split second later he felt a jab as the baby kicked several times against his palm.

"Whoa!" Dylan exclaimed, astonished by the power behind the kicks. "That's amazing! Does this go on all the time?" he asked, bringing his gaze back to hers.

Maggie's breath caught in her throat when she saw the look of genuine interest in his eyes. A moment ago as he'd waited to feel the baby move, his touch had seemed almost impersonal. But all at once she was aware of the warmth from his hand spreading through her, arousing forgotten sensations.

The intimacy of sharing such a powerful moment, of having him feel the life growing inside her, a life he'd helped create, was suddenly too much.

Maggie took a step back, breaking the contact. "Excuse me, I'll go and look for those photographs," she said, forcing the words past the ball of emotion clogging her throat.

Without waiting for a reply, she retreated around the table, and careful to avoid looking at Dylan, made her way from the kitchen.

Dylan stood for a long moment staring after Maggie's departing figure. With a muttered curse he began to clear the dishes from the table.

As he loaded the dishwasher his thoughts lingered on those breath-stealing seconds when he'd actually felt the baby...his baby, move.

Not for the first time since Maggie had dropped that bombshell on him, Dylan experienced an uneasy and uncomfortable feeling, a feeling that set off an alarm somewhere inside him.

Strangely enough, he was convinced she had spoken the truth when she'd said he was the father of her child, but he sensed a wariness, a caution in Maggie that somehow led him to wonder anew about the relationship they'd shared.

He was relying on his instincts, of course, but so far, his instincts had served him well. And while there were a growing number of questions he needed to know the answers to, the situation itself was, to say the least, somewhat delicate.

Dylan closed the dishwasher and, crossing to the French doors leading to the porch, stepped outside. Taking a deep breath, he gazed up at the evening sky.

If only he could remember! If only— Dylan brought his thoughts to a halt. Maybe Maggie was right, maybe he was trying too hard.

"Here's the album!"

Dylan reentered the kitchen in time to see her drop the small photo album on the table before going to the sink.

"Would you like a cup of tea?" she asked. Lifting the small kettle from the top of the stove, she filled it from the water tap.

"Yes, thank you." Dylan reached over to pick up the album. Flipping the book open, he sat down and slowly began to leaf through the photographs.

From her vantage point at the sink, Maggie darted

a quick glance at Dylan, holding her breath in anticipation, as he carefully studied each picture.

"The bride and groom look very happy," he commented as he returned to the beginning of the book.

Maggie tensed. "They *were* happy," she mumbled under her breath, noisily dropping the kettle onto the stove to cover her words.

Dylan glanced up at her and frowned. "I'm sorry. Did you say something?"

"No," Maggie replied, keeping her back to him. Opening the cupboard door, she pulled out two cups and saucers, annoyed with herself for reacting.

But she remembered quite vividly, as they'd stood together watching his aunt and her father drive off on their honeymoon, Dylan's pronouncement that he very much doubted the marriage would last.

Shocked, Maggie had asked Dylan what he had against marriage, only to be told that anyone who depended solely on another person for their happiness was a fool. Then he'd added that as far as he was concerned, marriage was one institution he had no intention of ever joining.

Chapter Four

Maggie had never forgotten Dylan's caustic comment on his feelings about marriage, nor his parting words the morning after they'd made love, words that had come back to haunt her with painful regularity throughout her pregnancy.

When the kettle on the stove whistled its readiness, she filled the delicate china teapot and set it on the tray.

"Here, let me get that," Dylan offered, crossing to the counter.

Maggie didn't protest, warmed by his thoughtfulness and silently acknowledging that his manners and strong sense of chivalry were two of the characteristics she'd found most endearing about him.

Dylan depositing the tray on the table and resumed his seat. "That lawyer fellow," he began.

"Jared." Maggie supplied her friend's name, as she proceeded to fill the cups.

Dylan nodded. "Right...Jared gave me the impression my aunt and your father had taken a number of trips since their wedding.''

Maggie lowered herself into the chair opposite and slid a cup and saucer toward Dylan. "They did," she confirmed. "As soon as they got back from their honeymoon, they invested in a small motor home. They called it their home away from home. It wasn't long before they headed off on one of many cross-country tours," Maggie added.

She smiled to herself, recalling how much her father and Rosemary had enjoyed being on the road, exploring new places and meeting new people.

Dylan added milk to his tea and slowly stirred the contents, a frown on his face. "But weren't they in a plane crash when—" He stopped the instant he saw the tears pooling in Maggie's eyes. "I'm sorry," he hurried on, apologetically.

Maggie sniffed and blinked away the tears. "It's all right." Snatching a tissue from the box on the table, she summoned a weak smile. "At this stage of my pregnancy, weeping at the drop of a hat seems to be an occupational hazard."

In truth, her hormones were only partly to blame. During the first few weeks after her father's and Rosemary's deaths, she'd felt completely and utterly alone. Even now, she still felt a sharp sense of loss and missed them both, immeasurably.

When the doctor told her she was having a baby, she remembered quite clearly the feeling of pure joy that had spread through her, warming her soul. Somehow it had seemed so right that the tender yet explosive passion she and Dylan had shared that night had resulted in a child being conceived.

She'd hugged the secret to her, naively fostering

the hope that when he returned to Grace Harbor to claim his inheritance, she would tell him the results of their lovemaking, and he would sweep her into his arms and ask her to be his wife.

But weeks passed with no sign of him, weeks of waiting and hoping, weeks of worrying and wondering, until Maggie had been forced to face the truth. Dylan wasn't coming back, and the passionate encounter they'd shared meant nothing to him, and had simply evolved out of the pain of their mutual loss at a time when they'd both been emotionally vulnerable.

The ache in her heart had become unbearable, and all the harder to endure because she'd had no one to turn to, no one to talk to, no one to offer her comfort or support.

She'd been entirely alone—until she remembered the tiny baby growing inside her, the innocent child who needed her, whose life depended on her and whom she already loved with all her heart.

Dylan watched the array of emotions flitting across Maggie's features. That she was struggling to maintain control was obvious, but the look of abject sorrow he could see in the depths of her brown eyes caused a tightness in his chest.

"They were on their way to Bar Harbor in Maine to visit friends who were celebrating their fiftieth wedding anniversary," Maggie said at last, pushing aside her own pain-filled memories.

"They'd stopped in Wisconsin at a resort somewhere in the Dales," she continued. "My father called me from there saying they were having mechanical problems with the motor home. Instead of waiting for the repairs to be done, they decided to fly to Maine and surprise their friends.'' She stopped and swallowed several times before continuing.

"Apparently a storm had been forecast, but it turned out to be much more severe than first reported,'' she went on, managing to keep her tone even. "The small plane was hit by lightning and came down in dense brush.'' Her voice trailed off, and with hands that weren't quite steady she brought the teacup to her lips, hoping the hot liquid would help wash away the lump of emotion lodged in her throat.

"Maggie, I'm so sorry,'' Dylan said softly, hearing the raw pain in her voice. "It must have been difficult for you...dealing with that on your own....''

"I...I wasn't alone. At least—'' She faltered feeling her face grow warm. She flicked a glance at Dylan, but there was nothing in his expression that gave any indication their conversation had triggered a memory. Relieved, she hurried on. "You drove up from San Diego for the funeral.''

"Oh,'' Dylan said.

"But you had to leave early the next morning,'' she added.

"I don't remember any of it,'' Dylan said, with a shake of his head. When the doctors at the hospital finally told him about his aunt's death, he recalled quite vividly his feelings of utter despair. She'd been the only family he'd had apparently...the only person who could have helped him fill in at least some of his past.

Now he was alone... No! That wasn't strictly true. If Maggie's revelation earlier was to be believed, he would be a father very soon. Suddenly Dylan's mind filled with questions, questions only she could answer.

"Maggie, what about us—our relationship?" He heard her sharp intake of breath at the question and noted the flicker of some emotion, quickly controlled, in the depths of her eyes.

But before he could pursue the matter, the singsong chimes of the doorbell echoed through the silence.

"Oh...excuse me." Maggie rose from the table and made her escape, relieved beyond measure at the timely interruption. Dylan's question about their relationship had come out of the blue, and she'd had no idea how to answer him.

Opening the front door, Maggie found herself staring at the smiling faces of Richard and Beverly Chason.

"Richard! Bev!" Maggie tried to hide her surprise at finding the couple on her doorstep. Back in March she'd written them, letting them know of her decision not to open Fairwinds until later in the season, and asking if they'd mind changing their standing reservation for the first two weeks in June to later in the summer.

When she'd received no response to her letter, she'd placed several phone calls to their home in Gillette, Wyoming, again without success.

"Why, Maggie! You're having a baby. How wonderful! Don't tell me you've gone and got married on us." Beverly enveloped Maggie in a motherly hug.

Maggie's arms instinctively circled the older woman's small frame, and for the second time in as many minutes she felt the sting of tears in her eyes.

"No...I'm not married," Maggie said softly as Beverly withdrew.

"Oh, my dear, I'm sorry," Beverly said, and for a moment there was an awkward silence.

Richard set down the two suitcases he was carrying. "Congratulations, Maggie! When's the baby due?" he asked, gently pulling her into a warm embrace.

"June twenty-second." Maggie's tone was husky as tears filled her eyes once more at Richard's ready acceptance of her situation.

"That's only three weeks away," Beverly commented. "Are you keeping Fairwinds open until the baby's born?" she asked.

Maggie felt her face grow warm. "Actually, no. I wrote you a letter," she began and saw the couple exchange startled looks.

"A letter?" Beverly repeated, her face a picture of concern. "We didn't receive a letter. At least— Oh, Richard! I told you we should have called Maggie to confirm our reservation, but what with all the upheaval..." She broke off, a look of dismay on her face.

"Don't worry. It's all right," Maggie quietly assured them.

"I'm sorry, Maggie, Bev's right, we should have called," Richard said. "It's just that for the past three months we've been living in a hotel," he said. "Our house was damaged during a storm in February, and we had to move out while the repairs were being done."

"Your letter must have got lost in the shuffle," Beverly chipped in, offering the most likely explanation.

"As I said, it's not a problem," Maggie repeated with a warm smile. "You're welcome to stay. In fact,

I readied your room this morning, just in case," she told them. It had been Dylan's unexpected appearance that had wiped all thoughts of them from her mind.

"Are you sure?" Beverly asked, genuine concern in her voice. "We don't want to make extra work for you...what with the baby due."

"I'm positive," Maggie replied with a smile, noting the look of relief on both their faces.

"We promise not to be rowdy or keep you awake practicing our tap dancing while we're here," Richard said with a teasing smile.

Maggie chuckled softly. "Then it's a deal," she responded. "I've put you in your usual room."

"Thanks, Maggie," Beverly said flashing her a smile.

"I'm so glad you're here," Maggie said, and felt her throat close over with emotion.

"It's lovely to see you, too, dear," Beverly replied, and Maggie saw the glint of tears as the older woman reached out and squeezed Maggie's hand.

"Come along, darling. It's been a long drive and I'm exhausted." Richard gathered up the suitcases once more and headed for the stairs.

"Good night, Maggie. See you in the morning," Beverly said as she followed her husband.

Maggie locked the front door and made her way to the kitchen. A quick glance around told her the room was empty, and for a fleeting moment she wondered if Dylan had left, but she quickly dismissed the fanciful notion.

While the chime of the doorbell had proved a timely interruption, Maggie felt sure Dylan wouldn't let the matter of their previous relationship rest, and knew it wouldn't be long before he broached the subject again.

She was still at a loss to know how to answer his questions. What they'd shared could be described as a one-night stand, a passionate encounter or a brief torrid affair.

But for her the night spent in Dylan's arms had been wonderful and magical and a dream come true, because from the first moment she'd set eyes on Dylan at his aunt's wedding five years ago, she'd fallen hopelessly and helplessly in love with him.

And while things hadn't turned out quite how she'd imagined or hoped, she had no regrets.

For a moment Maggie recalled Richard and Beverly Chason's reaction to her announcement that she wasn't married.

She'd seen the glint of curiosity in Bev's eyes, and for a moment she'd half expected, even anticipated their disapproval. But instead they'd accepted the news without question, and Bev was much too polite to inquire about the identity of the baby's father.

When her pregnancy had become obvious, some of Grace Harbor's residents had eyed her with open disdain, tut-tutting and shaking their heads whenever they met her on the street, even crossing the street to avoid her.

Maggie had smiled through it all, ignoring the looks and comments thrown her way, though there had been times when she'd felt angry and hurt at their judgmental attitude.

"Have they gone?" Dylan's voice brought her out of her reverie and she turned to find him standing in the doorway leading onto the back stairs, a duffel bag in his hand.

"No. Actually, they're staying," Maggie told him.

"I thought you said Fairwinds wasn't open for business," he commented.

"It isn't," she responded. "But the Chasons have been regular customers ever since I started. I couldn't ask them to leave."

"I was thinking of staying awhile myself," he remarked. "Is that a problem?"

Maggie ignored the leap her heart took at his words. "No problem," she said. "Besides you do own half, or have you forgotten?" she said, her tone more sharp than she'd intended.

"I haven't forgotten," he replied, an answering edge to his voice. "Let's just say I haven't quite gotten used to the idea," he explained. "It's been rather an eventful day, and I'm tired. Perhaps you could point me in the direction of a suitable room."

Maggie stifled a sigh, annoyed with herself for her rudeness. He was right, it had been an eventful day. "I'm sorry," she mumbled the apology. "If you'd like to come this way."

Dylan followed Maggie from the kitchen. From his experience earlier outside the garage he felt reasonably sure he'd stayed at Fairwinds before, but nothing about the old house seemed at all familiar.

Ahead of him, Maggie glanced into a room on her left, and as he drew level with the open door, he darted a quick look inside.

He stopped to stare. Orange and black striped tigers, along with big-tusked elephants, black and white zebras and golden-maned lions wandered across the walls.

Suspended from the ceiling above a brightly colored baby change table were two monkeys, two antelopes and two giraffes.

A large cardboard box was leaning against one wall, and nearby stood a small dresser painted white. In the center of the room, on a braided oval rug, sat an old rocking chair.

"Wow!" Dylan said, as he crossed the threshold.

Maggie turned in time to see Dylan disappear inside the baby's room. Instantly her pulse gathered speed as she retraced her steps.

"Did you decorate the room yourself?" he asked when she appeared in the doorway.

"Yes." Maggie was aware as she entered that it suddenly seemed smaller, due, she felt sure, to Dylan's tall imposing presence.

"You've done a great job," he told her, his tone sincere.

"Thank you." She tried to ignore the warmth spreading through her at his compliment.

"Is that the crib?" He pointed to the large cardboard box.

"Yes," Maggie said. "It needs to be assembled."

"You shouldn't be doing heavy work like that in your condition. I'd be happy to put it together for you."

Maggie met his gaze, surprised and strangely moved by the offer.

"Thank you," she said after a brief hesitation.

"You didn't answer my question earlier," Dylan said, his tone changing now.

"Question?" Maggie felt her mouth go dry knowing with growing apprehension exactly where he was heading.

"About our relationship." Dylan immediately

caught the flicker of alarm that came and went in her eyes. "When did we become involved? How long had we been lovers?"

Maggie's heart jolted against her rib cage. Bravely she met his gaze and was immediately held captive by his piercing gray eyes boring into hers, as if he was trying to see inside her head.

Sensing her unease, the baby began to kick repeatedly, adding to her discomfort and increasing the tension vibrating through her. It was all Maggie could do not to turn and head for the safety and sanctuary of her room.

Silently she willed herself to remain calm, and as the baby's kicks gradually subsided she tried to think of a suitable answer to his question.

She was tempted for a brief moment to concoct a story, a romantic tale of how they'd fallen madly in love the first time they'd met, while standing at the altar the day her father had married his aunt.

But while it might have been a true rendering of what had happened, at least from her standpoint, in all honesty she had no idea how Dylan had felt about her then or later, for that matter.

"We...I..." She ground to a halt. Dragging her eyes from his, she took a step back. She drew a steadying breath, all the while ignoring the way her heart was hammering like a wild thing inside her breast. "We met—" She tried to swallow but couldn't.

Should she tell him that there hadn't really been a relationship between them? Should she explain that the only time they'd been lovers had been that night a little over eight months ago when they'd been dealing with a tragic loss, leaving them both in a highly vulnerable state?

"I'm sorry, I don't feel well," she said, and in truth she was beginning to feel nauseous. "Would you mind very much if we did this another time?" Tiredness had seeped into her voice.

Dylan was silent for a long moment, and Maggie could feel his frustration. "Of course," he said at last and Maggie almost sagged with relief.

"Your room is this way," she said, and led him into the hallway.

A little farther down the hall she opened the door to the small guest room, the room Dylan had used on previous occasions when he'd stayed at Fairwinds.

"The bedroom has its own bathroom," she told him as she stood back to allow him access. "Oh...and you'll find clean towels in the bathroom closet," she added.

"Thank you." Dylan edged past Maggie and as he did, his arm briefly brushed against her abdomen. The fleeting contact sent a ripple of response skidding up her spine, robbing her of breath.

"Good night," she managed to say, her voice sounding husky.

"Good night," Dylan replied, but she was already heading to her own room.

Once inside she leaned heavily against the door, taking several deep, steadying breaths, telling herself her reaction had nothing to do with Dylan, but was simply a result of static electricity from the hall carpet.

She walked to the window and stood for a moment enjoying the cool summer breeze that carried in the sweet, delicate fragrance of the roses in the flower bed below.

How many times had she stood in this exact spot,

staring up at the stars, wishing with all her heart for Dylan to come back to her and make all her dreams come true?

Her wish had come true...at least part of it. Dylan had come back. But as for making all her dreams come true...

Chapter Five

Maggie stood at the stove preparing breakfast for the Chasons. Bacon sizzled in the frying pan, its strong aroma making her stomach churn.

She could feel small beads of perspiration forming on her forehead, and she inhaled deeply, trying to fight off the wave of sickness threatening to overtake her.

"Mmm...there's nothing like the smell of bacon cooking to entice a person out of bed." The voice startled her, and her pulse skittered wildly. She glanced over her shoulder to see Dylan, his hair still damp from the shower, wearing faded blue jeans and a white T-shirt.

Awareness sharp and unwelcome intensified the symptoms she was struggling to control. "Good morning," she managed to say before returning to her task.

"Are you feeling all right? You look a little pale."

His voice was closer now, and she sensed he was standing directly behind her.

She could feel the warmth radiating from his body, and as she drew a steadying breath, she was assailed with his familiar masculine scent. Her knees wobbled and threatened to buckle beneath her.

"Oh…" Her exclamation came out in a rush of air, and if Dylan hadn't been there to take her weight, she would surely have fallen.

"Whoa…I've got you," Dylan said. His strong arms held her firm, and even in her dizzy state Maggie felt his muscles tense as he braced to steady her.

His breath fanned her cheek, and her heart tripped over itself in a flurry of response. Closing her eyes, she gave herself up to the sweet joy of being held in his arms.

"You'd better sit down," he said as he practically carried her to the nearest kitchen chair.

Once she was safely seated, he released her, and Maggie almost whimpered in protest, biting back the sigh of longing trembling on her lips.

"What happened?" Dylan asked as he crouched in front of her.

"Morning sickness," Maggie managed to respond.

"Morning sickness," Dylan repeated.

"It usually only happens in the early stages of pregnancy," she said. "But during the past month, I've had a few bouts with it," she told him. "I'll be all right in a minute. Oh…the bacon…it'll burn—" She attempted to get up, but Dylan quickly forestalled her.

"I'll get it." He rose and returned to the stove.

"Are you cooking this for me?" Dylan asked after he'd removed the frying pan from the heat.

"Yes...well, you and the Chasons," Maggie replied. "They like to have breakfast around eight." She glanced at the clock on the wall. "It's almost that now," she added with a hint of anxiety.

"Stay where you are," Dylan ordered. "You still look a little green around the gills." He softened his words with a teasing grin. "I'll take care of breakfast. Just tell me what's left to do," he said.

Maggie's heart fluttered in her breast in reaction to his grin, and somehow she couldn't summon the energy to reject his offer of help.

"Thanks," Maggie said. "Uh...there's scrambled eggs keeping warm in the oven," she told him. "You just need to toast a few slices of bread. Coffee and orange juice are already in the dining room."

"No problem! Toast coming right up," Dylan said, reaching for the bread box.

A light knock on the swing door leading to the small dining room brought Maggie's head around.

"Good morning, Maggie." The greeting came from Beverly Chason who'd poked her head around the door. "Oh—sorry, I didn't mean to interrupt," she said when she saw Dylan. "I thought I'd see if you needed any help."

"Morning, Bev," Maggie responded with a smile. "Thanks for the offer, but everything is under control. I'd like you to meet my business partner, Dylan O'Connor. Dylan, this is Beverly Chason."

"I'm very pleased to meet you, Mr. O'Connor," Beverly said with a polite nod of her head.

"The pleasure's mine," Dylan replied with an easy charm. "Please, call me Dylan. I'll be your waiter this morning," he went on. "If you'd care to take a seat, I'll bring your breakfast through in a few moments.''

"Oh…that's lovely. Thank you,'' Beverly responded and, flashing a smile at Maggie, quietly withdrew.

Maggie watched in fascination as Dylan served up breakfast. Carrying a plate in each hand, he nudged open the swing door with his shoulder and disappeared into the dining room.

Suddenly Maggie's nausea was replaced with the need to eat. Rising from the chair, she moved to the counter to drop two pieces of bread into the toaster.

She could hear the murmur of voices coming from the dining room. Reaching for the jug of orange juice, she poured herself a glass, and when the toast was done she spread a layer of peanut butter on it.

"Feeling better?'' Dylan asked as he rejoined her in the kitchen.

"Much better,'' she assured him. "Thanks for your help.''

"No problem. After all, we are business partners.'' Returning to the stove, Dylan served up a plate of scrambled eggs and bacon.

"Are you up to eating some of this?'' he asked, glancing at her.

"Toast is just fine for me,'' she said. "Would you like some?''

"Stay where you are. I'll get it.''

A few moments later he joined Maggie at the kitchen table. "The Chasons are a nice couple,'' Dylan commented, as he bit into a piece of bacon. "They told me they met fifty years ago right here in Grace Harbor, and come back each year to celebrate their anniversary,'' Dylan said.

"That's right," Maggie said.

"They've been together a long time," he commented.

"Oh...they haven't been married fifty years," Maggie said.

"They haven't?" Dylan replied with a frown.

"Bev's parents didn't approve of Richard or the relationship," Maggie said. "They kept them apart for ten years."

"Ten years! You're joking!" Dylan said between mouthfuls.

"Beverly's parents had plans for their daughter," Maggie said, relating the story she'd heard from the Chasons the first time they'd stayed at Fairwinds. "Plans that didn't include a young man of dubious background, a young man of twenty-one, a man they considered beneath their standing."

Dylan reached for a piece of toast. "It's hard to believe that kind of thing really happened," he commented wryly as he spread jam on his toast. "How did they find each other again?"

Maggie rose from the chair and carried her glass to the dishwasher. "If you ask Richard and Bev that question they'll tell you it was fate—that they met again because they were destined to be together."

"Fate...destiny..." Dylan repeated the words with a smile. "Rather romantic ideas, don't you think? I'm not sure I subscribe to that philosophy," he commented.

"You don't believe fate could bring two people together, that they could be destined for each other?" Maggie held her breath waiting for his answer.

The Dylan she'd known before the accident would have instantly dismissed the sentimentality of such a notion, but there was no mistaking the fact that the man before her obviously found the idea intriguing.

"I will say this." His tone was thoughtful. "Ever since I arrived here, ever since I bumped into you in the street yesterday, I can't help thinking that something, be it fate or destiny, brought me here."

A shiver chased down Maggie's spine at his words. "I thought you said you found a letter from Jared," she countered, wanting to put things back on a more solid footing.

"True," Dylan responded easily. "But I could have simply chosen to write Jared or call him on the phone. I didn't have to drive all this way. My instincts were telling me to come here, and ever since my arrival things have started happening, especially here in this house, that make me believe my memory will come back one day."

Maggie's heart skidded to a halt. "You mean there's a chance your memory won't come back?" she asked.

"From what little I've been told, the odds are against it," Dylan said. "Only one of the doctors in San Diego even encouraged me to make the trip, the others said I shouldn't try to force myself to remember...that I should accept what happened and just get on with my life."

"I see," Maggie said, hearing the hint of despair in his voice. "When are you due back at the base?" she asked, wondering how long he planned to stay. But before Dylan could respond the swing door to the dining room opened and Richard appeared.

"Excuse the interruption," he said easily. "We thought we'd tell you we're on our way out."

"Would you like me to prepare a lunch for you to take with you?" Maggie asked.

"Thanks, Maggie. But we'll have lunch out today," he said.

"Have a nice day," Maggie said.

"What do they find to do around here?" Dylan asked, once Richard had left.

"They love to sail or hike and they're keen bird watchers," she told him. "They also visit several friends who live in and around the area," Maggie said.

"That was delicious," Dylan said as he gathered up his plate.

"What are your plans for the day?" Maggie asked, wondering if he planned to be underfoot.

"Your lawyer friend mentioned that the back stairs were in need of repair. I thought I'd take a closer look at them today. Have you seen about getting an estimate?" he asked.

"No," she responded. "I've been putting it off, mostly because Jared told me any repairs would need to be approved by both of us."

"I see," Dylan said, as he washed his hands at the sink. "Well, who knows, maybe I can figure out what needs to be done."

"You think you can fix them?" Maggie asked in surprise.

Dylan flashed her a smile that sent her heart into a tailspin. "I have no idea," he said. "But I'll soon find out." With that he headed toward the French doors leading to the deck.

Maggie spent the next half hour clearing away the dishes and returning the kitchen and dining room to their usual state of tidiness.

She could hear Dylan outside on the stairs, and wondered again when he had to report for duty. In all probability, due to the injuries he'd sustained, he was still on medical leave. But he'd seemed reluctant to answer her question earlier and had looked relieved when Richard appeared.

Maggie frowned. The navy was Dylan's whole life. He'd joined up soon after he'd graduated from high school, and Rosemary had once said that his ambition had been to climb to the top.

Rosemary had sung her nephew's praises to such an extent throughout the two weeks leading up to her marriage to Maggie's father that Maggie had been eager to meet the man Rosemary held in such high regard, just to see for herself if he cut as dashing a picture as Rosemary had painted.

Maggie hadn't been disappointed. In fact, if the truth were known, she'd fallen hard the moment she'd seen him walking down the aisle in his immaculate dress uniform, with Rosemary on his arm.

Her father had asked Maggie to stand with him at the front of the church, saying he needed her by his side, that he wanted her to be his "best man."

Though the arrangement had been a little unorthodox, Reverend Stanley had been most accommodating, knowing that ever since Maggie's mother's death, her father had devoted himself to his daughter.

At the small reception after the service, Maggie had been seated next to Dylan, and though she'd tried to draw him out, tried to make him notice her, even tried to flirt with him, he'd seemed less than interested.

Not that he'd been rude, his manners had been impeccable, yet she'd sensed a reservedness, an aloofness, as if he was hiding behind a protective shield.

She'd casually mentioned this when she'd gone to help Rosemary get ready to leave for her honeymoon, and been surprised at the tears that appeared in the other woman's eyes.

Rosemary had told her she'd tried, without success, to knock down the barrier Dylan had erected as a protection against the world. Maggie remembered feeling sad as she'd listened to Rosemary recount how Dylan, at the age of two, had been abandoned by his mother.

Foster homes had followed, and because the authorities hadn't been able to track down Dylan's mother and get her consent to have him put up for adoption, he'd been bounced around for the next twelve years.

Rosemary had told Maggie that during the time he'd lived with her, she'd caught glimpses of the warm and loving young man he seemed determined to keep hidden. Rosemary had also said that she hoped one day, a loving, generous and perceptive woman would come along and melt the wall he'd built around his heart.

It had been later, as Rosemary and William waved goodbye to their small group of friends, that Dylan had voiced his opinion on marriage, but while Maggie had been shocked by his remarks, she'd remembered his aunt's comments.

"Your lawyer friend is right," Dylan's deep resonant voice cut through Maggie's reflections.

"About what?" she asked, turning to face him, noting his thoughtful expression, as if he was trying to mentally work out a problem.

"The stairs are in a bad way," he told her. "In fact I'd recommend, no make that insist, that you stay off them altogether. The railing is loose and in danger of giving way, and most of the risers are rotting. It all needs to be torn down and replaced.''

"Are you sure?'' Maggie responded, surprised not only to learn the damage was so extensive, but that Dylan sounded confident and appeared to know what he was talking about.

She'd been aware of the loose handrail, it had been wobbly for some time, as for the steps, she hadn't noticed anything untoward other than the odd creaking sound.

"I'm very sure,'' he replied. "I'm wondering where I could have learned basic carpentry. I suspect I must have taken a course in construction during my training, because I knew exactly what and where to look.''

"I'll have to check in the phone book and find someone to come and give an estimate on the cost of replacing the stairs,'' said Maggie. "Do you have any idea how expensive it will be?''

"Just the cost of materials,'' came Dylan's quick response.

"Materials? But—''

"I'll rebuild the stairs,'' he calmly assured her. "All I need is a tape measure and a pad of paper.''

"I can't say I've ever seen stairs made out of a tape measure and paper before,'' Maggie commented, unable to resist teasing him.

Dylan's eyes flashed to hers, and for several heart-stopping seconds their gazes locked. The smile that slowly began to spread over his features eradicated, at least temporarily, the lines of pain and worry so evident around his eyes and mouth.

"Oh…very funny,'' Dylan drawled.

Maggie heard the humor lacing his voice and felt her heart skip a beat in instant response.

"Uh...there should be a tape measure in the second drawer of the hutch, and there's a notepad by the phone," she told him, hoping he wouldn't notice the breathless note in her voice.

"Thanks." Dylan moved to the oak hutch near the door leading to the dining room.

"It won't take long to figure out how much lumber I'll need," he said.

"Are you really going to tackle the stairs yourself?" Maggie asked.

"Yes," he answered. "I'm sure I can do it." He ran a hand through his hair. "At least that's what my instincts are telling me. And I wouldn't mind finding out if I'm right."

The look of determination in his eyes had darkened them to slate gray, and there was an air of excitement about him reminiscent of a young boy eager to show off a newfound skill.

"Fine," Maggie said, and saw the flicker of relief in his eyes.

"Can you point me to the nearest lumberyard?" he asked.

"Go down Indigo to Main Street and turn right," she said. "Keep driving until you get to the edge of town. You'll see the sign for Jerry's Lumber. You can't miss it," she told him.

"Thanks." He strode to the French doors and stopped. "Oh...I'd keep these doors locked. I'm pretty sure the deck itself is safe but, it might be best to avoid using it, at least for the time being." His tone left her with little doubt as to the serious nature of the warning.

"Fine," she said. Although she used the stairs almost every day to access the garage and her small vegetable garden, she acknowledged that it would be foolish for her to take any chances.

"I'm not trying to alarm you. But for your own sake and the baby's, better safe than sorry," Dylan said before pulling the door closed behind him.

Maggie stood staring after Dylan for a long moment. There had been no mistaking the emotion in his voice. His concern warmed her and sent her spirits rising.

"I think he just might care about you," she said softly as she massaged her abdomen, and when the baby kicked at her somewhat playfully in response, Maggie smiled.

Had Dylan gotten over the shock of learning he was the father of her baby? The fact that he hadn't denounced her declaration or challenged it, seemed to indicate that he believed she was telling the truth.

Would the old Dylan have acted the same? Somehow she doubted it. Perhaps his memory loss had also eradicated the wall he'd built around himself and his emotions.

Suddenly she found herself wondering what his reaction would be when she told him their relationship had been nothing more than a one-night stand.

Maggie flinched at her own harsh description of what, for her, had been a night of pure magic. Dylan had been a different man then, too. She'd seen a softer, vulnerable side of him, a side she hadn't been able to resist.

But while she accepted half the blame for what had happened between them, she also admitted she'd been blinded by her own romantic hopes and dreams concerning Dylan, and knew she'd been naive to assume her feelings for him were reciprocated.

With a sigh Maggie pushed these thoughts aside and headed upstairs to the Chasons' room and for the next half hour she busied herself tidying up and putting fresh towels in the bathroom.

An hour later Maggie was sitting contentedly on the grass verge adjoining her small vegetable garden, tugging at the fresh crop of weeds, when she heard the sound of a car in the driveway.

With earth-covered fingers, she nudged the wide brim of her straw hat out of her face and glanced around in time to see Dylan emerge from behind the wheel of his car.

She resolutely refused to acknowledge the jittery leap her pulse made at the sight of him striding across the lawn toward her.

"Did you find the lumberyard?" she asked, squinting up into the sun.

Dylan crouched to her level, resting his tanned forearms on his muscled thighs. "Yes," he replied. "The delivery truck will be by a little later to drop off the wood I ordered," he told her.

"Oh…that's great," she said.

"I forgot to ask you if there are any tools in the garage," he said. "I'm assuming your father had some, but maybe you've disposed of them…"

"No. I've been meaning to clean out his workshop and sell his tools…but I haven't gotten around to it. I don't know if you'll find what you want, but I'll show you what there is," she said. Placing her hand on the grass beside her, she attempted to stand up.

"Let me help." Dylan straightened, then extended his hand.

Maggie stared for several breathless seconds at his muscled forearm. She was glad the wide brim of her hat hid her face and he couldn't see the color rising up her neck.

"Uh...I can manage," she said, aware that her heart was thundering in her ears. "Besides, my hands are dirty—" She fumbled over the excuse.

"A little dirt never hurt anyone," Dylan commented, bending closer as he spoke. "Here, grab my arm."

Maggie felt her mouth go dry and wished fervently she'd disobeyed Dylan's orders and gone out to the porch to retrieve the small stool she used whenever she felt the urge to weed the garden.

Sitting on the grass, especially in her present condition, had been a foolish move. But when she'd seen the tangle of weeds choking her carrots and lettuce plants she'd immediately felt it her duty to intervene.

Getting down hadn't been all that difficult. But getting back up did pose a problem. It was silly to try and avoid touching him. After all, he was merely offering his hand...the same hand she'd pressed to her abdomen in order for him to feel the baby move.

"Ah... Thank you." Maggie placed her hand on Dylan's arm and immediately felt his muscles tense as he braced himself for her weight. Strong fingers gripped her other hand, and her breath caught in her throat.

Once she had one foot planted firmly on the grass, she felt his arm slide around her waist for added support, and it was all she could do to suppress the shiver of longing that scurried down her spine.

For a man who'd recently been in a coma, a man she knew was not at his physical best, he helped her to her feet with startling ease.

As he steadied her, their gazes locked and for a mind-blowing second heat spiraled through her veins, leaving a trail of need in its wake. Their bodies were still touching, the baby gently pressed against Dylan's lean frame, and for the life of her Maggie couldn't move.

They stood transfixed, like two porcelain figures locked forever in a sensual embrace. Her pulse hammered a wild rhythm against her breast, while her heart seemed to be dancing a jig.

Suddenly the sharp blast of a horn shattered the spell, making them jump apart like two guilty teenagers. Dylan glanced over his shoulder at the source of the sound.

"It's the truck from the lumberyard," he said. "I'd better go and make sure they brought everything." He was already moving away. "Will you be all right?" he asked.

Maggie blinked. "Yes...yes, of course," she assured him with a smile, though her body kept insisting it would never be all right, not until he was holding her in his arms once again.

Chapter Six

Maggie stood for a moment waiting for her heartbeat to return to its normal pace. With slow, measured steps, she crossed the stretch of lawn separating the vegetable garden from her father's workshop.

She glanced briefly at Dylan and the truck driver unloading the dozen or more two-by-fours from the deck of the truck, as well as a number of wider planks she guessed would be used to replace the rotting stair risers.

When Maggie reached the shady overhang of the workshop she let out a sigh, glad to be out of the midday sun. Retrieving the key from its hook above the door, she let herself inside.

Maggie flicked on the light and stood for a moment staring at the long workbench against the far wall. Above it hung an array of chisels, wrenches and screwdrivers of various types and sizes.

The stronger smell of gasoline mingled with the

scents of sawdust and grease, and suddenly images of her father working at his bench flashed into her mind.

Her throat closed over with emotion, and her eyes filled with tears, as a host of memories engulfed her. A lawyer by day, her father had loved to relax and while away his evenings in his workshop, tinkering with bits and pieces of his old Model T engine, painstakingly rebuilding and restoring the car to its original state.

After clearing away the supper dishes, Maggie would wander out to the workshop, hop up onto the bench and watch. On warm summer evenings she'd bring him a glass of iced lemonade, lingering to chat about her hopes and dreams for the future.

"So…this is your father's workshop."

At the sound of Dylan's voice behind her, Maggie quickly brushed away her tears with the back of her hand, before turning to face him.

"Yes," she responded, ignoring the quicksilver leap of her pulse.

"Well, it's easy to see he was a tidy man," Dylan commented, his gaze sweeping around the workshop, noting the wide range of tools.

He took several steps toward her, and Maggie felt her heart flutter in alarm.

"My father liked to be organized," Maggie explained, a trifle breathlessly. "A place for everything and everything in its place…was his favorite expression," she added with a nervous smile.

Dylan made no comment. He was inspecting the contents of a tall row of wooden drawers standing next to the bench. Each drawer was clearly labeled with the size and type of nail or screw occupying its space.

He smiled and shook his head in silent admiration of William Fairchild's neatness. "Amazing," he said. "I'm sure I'll find whatever I need."

"Good," Maggie said, beginning to feel more than a little claustrophobic.

Intent on putting some space between them, she turned and took a step toward the door leading through to the garage, only to walk directly into a dust-covered cobweb, dangling from the ceiling.

Startled, she let out a soft moan at the same time waving frantically at the gossamer threads clinging to her face and hair.

Dylan instantly came to her aid, sweeping away the cobwebs with easy efficiency.

"Thank you," Maggie mumbled above the roar of her heartbeat, annoyed at her childish reaction and wishing now she hadn't come into the workshop at all. She eased away from him once more.

"Hold on a second!" Dylan ordered.

Maggie froze. Her heart shuddered to a halt as he stroked her cheek with the pad of his thumb. His touch, though fleeting, sent a quiver of need racing through her.

"There...it's gone." He flashed her a smile.

Mesmerized by the silvery glint in his eyes, Maggie felt a tingling warmth spread through her, leaving a trail of need behind.

The baby chose that moment to land a series of short, sharp kicks low in her abdomen. Grateful for the distraction, Maggie dropped her gaze and patted her stomach. "Hey, take it easy in there," she scolded, all the while trying to marshal her scattered thoughts.

"Active is he?" Dylan asked.

"With a vengeance," Maggie replied, relieved that the tension she'd felt a moment ago seemed to have dissipated. She started to move past Dylan.

"If it's all right with you," Dylan began. "I thought I'd start work on the stairs right away."

"Oh...sure...that's fine," Maggie replied, heading for the door.

"Might as well make myself useful," Dylan commented as he followed her.

"It's lunchtime," Maggie said. "Would you like to come in and eat now, or shall I bring you out a tray?"

"Don't go to any trouble on my account," he said. "I'll get started on the stairs and grab something later."

"Fine," Maggie said before slipping outside.

Dylan caught the door before it closed and stood watching until Maggie disappeared around the corner of the house.

A moment ago, when he'd gazed into her eyes, he'd been aware of the tension shimmering between them, a tension that was unmistakably sexual. And when he'd brushed away the stray cobwebs from her cheek, a sensation much like a tiny electric shock had sprinted through him, scrambling his senses.

The urge to close the gap between them and crush her mouth with his had been almost overwhelming, and not for the first time he wondered about the relationship they'd shared.

Last night, when he'd brought up the subject, he'd seen the look of panic that had flashed in her eyes. She'd pleaded tiredness and evaded the issue. But tempted though he'd been to pursue it, he'd backed off, unwilling to upset her, especially in her present condition.

Questions continued to plague him. If they'd been intimately involved over a period of time, it was reasonable to assume they'd exchanged phone calls or letters, which would have resulted in someone at the base knowing of his involvement with her.

He'd found no letters or photographs in his quarters, and no one had even mentioned the subject of him having a girlfriend. While he felt sure Maggie was telling the truth, that he was the baby's father, he was at a loss to understand why there appeared to be no evidence to support that they'd even had a relationship.

Perhaps they'd been on the verge of breaking up. Had she told him about the baby? Had she told him and he'd decided to walk away?

Dylan sagged against the door, weighed down by the questions he couldn't answer and fearful he'd hit the nail on the head. Was he really the kind of man who could walk away from such a responsibility? Dammit! He wished he knew the answer.

"Don't try to rush things. Take one day at a time. Time is a great healer." Doctor Bradford had repeated these phrases over and over to him during their sessions, and while time was something Dylan had plenty of…he sensed a strong resistance in Maggie to even talk about the relationship they'd shared.

With a sigh Dylan reached for a hammer and crowbar hanging from a hook on the wall and headed for the back stairs.

Maggie went to the kitchen window that overlooked the back stairs, but she could see no sign of

Dylan.

He'd been working steadily for the past two hours, stopping only long enough to eat the chicken sandwich and drink the pitcher of iced tea she'd left for him on the picnic table.

Up until now she'd resisted the urge to watch him at work, but, needing to satisfy her curiosity and see for herself the extent of the damage done to him in the car crash, she'd ambled to the window just in time to see him discard his sweat-stained T-shirt.

At the sight of his broad, lightly tanned, naked chest glistening with perspiration, her heart had instantly tripped into high gear.

There were no visible scars on his torso that she could see, but she was really too far away to be sure. The last time she'd seen Dylan in a similar state of undress had been the night they'd sought comfort in each other's arms, the night they'd made love, the night their child had been conceived.

As these memories flowed through her, she felt a shiver chase down her spine, and her body stirred in eager and urgent response.

Captivated by the sheen of sweat coating his rippling muscles, she watched him return to the task of demolishing the stairs. He wrestled with yet another step, his arms straining with the effort, and when the rotted wood finally gave way, he stumbled back and studied the results.

With the back of his hand, he wiped the sweat from his forehead, then perhaps sensing he had an audience, he glanced up at the window.

Like a guilty child caught with her hand in the

cookie jar, Maggie withdrew, but not before she'd seen the flash of his smile.

Annoyed at herself, she retreated to her room, where she spent an hour in bed staring at the ceiling, listening to the muted sounds of Dylan at work and trying to convince herself that her reactions were a result of her overloaded hormones, nothing more.

Boredom and hunger forced her to return to the kitchen, and when she heard the peal of the front doorbell, she knew it had to be Dylan.

"It isn't locked," Maggie said as she opened the front door. But when she saw Dylan standing on the doorstep looking dazed and confused, concern for him swamped her. "Are you hurt?" she asked, her tone urgent as she stepped toward him.

Dylan didn't hear Maggie's question or feel her hand on his arm. From the moment he'd turned the corner of the house and breathed in the sweet scent of the roses growing in the flower beds, a chill had swept through him, followed instantly by dizziness and nausea.

His reaction was almost identical to the one he'd experienced yesterday when the pain in his head and flashing images had sent him to his knees.

Convinced the two incidents were connected, Dylan tried to contain the excitement racing through him.

"What is it? What's wrong?" Maggie asked.

"Remember when you had to help me inside yesterday?" he said.

"Yes."

"As I approached the front door just now I suddenly started to feel dizzy, just like I did yesterday," he explained.

"What could be causing it?" she asked.

"I wish I knew," Dylan said, as the symptoms began to fade.

Could it have been a memory trying to surface? he wondered. He closed his eyes, praying silently for the return of the images he'd seen the previous day, but there was only a dark emptiness. Disappointment brought a bitter taste to his mouth.

"Dylan?"

He opened his eyes and saw Maggie's worried expression and silently berated himself for being the cause of it.

"I'm sorry, Maggie. It's nothing. I've probably just been out in the sun too long." He squeezed her hand and moved past her into the house. "What I need is a long, cool shower and a ten-minute power nap," he said.

"Take your time, there's no hurry," Maggie said, relieved he appeared to have shaken off the dizziness. "We'll have supper whenever you're ready," she added as he headed down the hall to his room.

Maggie closed the front door and returned to the kitchen. She busied herself chopping up a cabbage, green onions and an apple to make coleslaw, then opened a can of pineapple slices to garnish the ham steaks waiting to be cooked.

After she finished setting two places at the table, she wandered down the hall into the baby's room. Just as she settled herself comfortably in the rocking chair, the telephone rang.

Returning to the kitchen she picked up the receiver on the fifth ring. "Hello!" she said, her voice a little breathless.

"Maggie. Hi! It's me, Jared. Sorry...did I drag you away from something?"

"Jared. Hi. It's nice to hear from you," Maggie said. "No...I was just down the hall. How are you?"

"Busy, always busy" came the reply. "I meant to call you last night, but I've been..."

"Busy," Maggie supplied the word.

Jared laughed. "Right... Uh...correct me if I'm wrong, but you do know that Dylan O'Connor is in town and that he dropped by my office yesterday?"

"Yes. Why?" Maggie asked.

"Do you know where I can reach him? He didn't say where he was staying, but I thought I'd check with you. Fairwinds seemed the most logical choice. Is he there?" Jared asked.

"Yes, he's here," Maggie said. "He's in the shower right now. I'll get him to call you."

"No, that's okay," Jared replied. "I know where I can reach him. Have the two of you had a chance to discuss or decide what you're going to do with Fairwinds?" he asked.

"He knows I'm not interested in selling," Maggie said. "I offered to buy him out."

"What did he say?" Jared asked.

"Not much," she replied. "He's had a look at the stairs and agrees with your assessment that they need replacing. In fact, he's already started working on them."

"You mean he's hired someone to do the repairs?" Jared inquired.

"No, he's doing it himself," Maggie said.

"Really," Jared said, sounding faintly surprised. "Sounds like he's planning to stick around for a while. Did he say how long?"

It was a question Maggie wouldn't have minded knowing the answer to herself. "I've no idea," she said. "Why?"

"I need his signature and yours on a couple of documents. Maybe you could mention that to him," Jared explained. "Or maybe I'll just drop by and pay you both a visit."

"You're welcome anytime, Jared, you know that...and Paula, too," Maggie said, referring to Jared's wife. "By the way, how is Paula? Is she still getting the odd bout of morning sickness?"

"Yes, much to her disgust." Jared's reply held a hint of frustration and something more.

Maggie frowned. "But she is all right? I mean she's not having any problems with her pregnancy?"

"No...no problems. But unlike you, my...wife doesn't appear to enjoy being pregnant," Jared confided with a sigh. "She's already wishing it was all over."

"*She* wishes it was over," Maggie said, puzzled by the tension in Jared's voice. "Tell her I'm first in line for the delivery room...she's got another four months to wait," Maggie teased.

"You tell her," Jared replied. "I'm liable to get something thrown at me if I even bring up the subject."

Maggie laughed, but beneath Jared's words she heard more than a little frustration. Maggie had only met Paula a few times, the first back in March, when Jared had surprised everyone in town by returning from his two-week winter vacation in Hawaii, accompanied by his new and pregnant wife.

Tongues had been wagging ever since, but being the only lawyer in Grace Harbor, Jared hadn't lost out on any business. In fact, if anything he seemed busier than ever.

"Please give her my best," Maggie said before replacing the receiver.

Turning, she spotted Dylan in the doorway, and her heart began to trip a little faster. "I didn't hear you," she said, hoping he wouldn't notice the blush warming her cheeks.

"Sorry...didn't mean to startle you." Dylan walked toward her. "What's for supper?"

Maggie's gaze was drawn to his shiny black hair, still wet from the shower, and she noted too as he closed the gap between them that the dark stubble of his beard had gone.

His jaw looked smooth and inviting, and beneath the scent of the spicy aftershave he used she could smell Dylan's strong masculine scent, and an ache, slow and warm, began to spread through her, igniting a need she hadn't felt in a long time.

She spun away, fearful he might see the longing in her eyes. "That was Jared on the phone," she said, her voice faintly husky. "He said he's going to need our signatures on a few documents, but he'll come by the house one day, if that's okay."

She was babbling and she knew it, but he was standing directly behind her now and his nearness was creating havoc with her senses.

"Fine," Dylan replied. "Can I give you a hand with anything?" he asked.

"Uh...no...well... Could you pour me a glass of milk?" she asked, sure he must hear the thunderous roar of her heart. "Help yourself to a beer, if you'd like one, or you're welcome to open a bottle of wine."

"Milk is fine," he said, moving away to the fridge.

Maggie drew a steadying breath and turned her attention to cooking the ham steaks.

"This coleslaw is delicious," Dylan said a little later as they sat at the table. "Do you serve your bed-and-breakfast customers evening meals, too?" he asked.

"Sometimes. But only for repeat or regular customers, like Richard and Bev," Maggie said. "More often than not, I recommend one of the local restaurants."

"So Grace Harbor is a busy place in the summer," Dylan said.

"Yes. It's always been a popular spot with tourists," Maggie said. "There's lots to do, especially if you have kids, and even if you don't," she added, as she watched Dylan push his empty plate aside.

"Did you spend your childhood here?" Dylan asked.

"Yes," Maggie replied.

"Then you must have lots of friends around town," he commented.

"I do and I don't," she answered. "Strangely enough, most of the kids I went to high school or college with have either married and moved away or moved to the big city to pursue a career."

"Why did you stay?"

"Because I like it here and I wanted to be close to my father. He'd been talking about opening up Fairwinds as a bed-and-breakfast before he retired, but after he met Rosemary he told me I'd have to run it for him. And that's what I did," she said.

"What about—" She'd been going to ask Dylan a

question about his youth, his past…a past he didn't remember.

"What about me? Is that what you were going to ask?" Dylan finished for her, his smile rueful. "I wish I could tell you.…"

"I'm sorry. I wasn't thinking," she said.

"Hey…it's all right." He pushed back his chair and stood up. Gathering up their plates, he carried them to the sink.

Maggie was silent as she watched Dylan rinse the plates then stack them in the dishwasher. She found herself thinking she could quite easily grow accustomed to having him around, permanently.

Her heart slammed against her rib cage at the thought. It was a pipe dream, nothing more. Dylan was the father of her baby and had every right to be a part of the baby's life, but unlike most couples whose relationship had gone through the various stages of development, from mutual attraction to courtship to marriage, theirs had been a brief encounter. They really hardly even knew each other, and she wondered if, when his memory returned, he would withdraw once again behind the protective wall he'd built around himself, and it would only be a matter of time before he walked away a second time.

"Maggie? Maggie…"

The sound of Dylan's voice penetrated her wayward thoughts. "Uh…sorry…I was miles away," she muttered.

"I was wondering if you had any aspirin," he said.

"Yes, in the medicine cabinet in the main bathroom," she told him. "Headache?" she asked.

Dylan smiled and shook his head. "Not ex-

actly...my muscles are aching. Not surprising after
the workout I put them through today."

"Oh...I see," Maggie responded, as Dylan disappeared down the hall to the bathroom.

Maggie folded the linen place mats and napkins
and put them away in the hutch. As she opened the
drawer, a napkin slid from her grasp and fell to the
floor.

"I'll get it," Dylan said, coming up behind her.
And before Maggie could move out of his way, he
quickly retrieved the fallen napkin and dropped it into
the drawer.

"Thanks," she said. "Picking things up off the
floor is becoming something of a problem these
days," she added with a smile.

"What if you'd fallen?" he asked, his tone suddenly serious.

"Then I probably would have lain there until Richard and Bev came back," she joked, but she could
see no answering humor in Dylan's eyes.

"Could a fall start your labor?" he asked.

"Yes, I suppose it's possible," she acknowledged.
"But I didn't fall," she said.

"Not this time," he agreed. "But accidents do happen, especially in the home, and often with disastrous
effects," he added.

Maggie couldn't quite meet his gaze. He was right.
Yesterday Dr. Whitney had asked her if she'd thought
about inviting a friend or relative to stay with her until
the baby was born, for just that reason.

"I didn't fall," she repeated, keeping her tone
light, wishing he'd move away. "And besides, if I
had fallen, you were here."

"That's not the point, Maggie..." He spoke softly,

his breath fanning her face. Touched by his show of concern, she felt her heart skip a beat.

"Excuse me," she said abruptly, suddenly needing to put some space between them. Dylan didn't budge.

"Stubborn little soul, aren't you?" His tone was tender and amused rather than angry, sending Maggie's blood racing through her veins. "I suppose in a small town like Grace Harbor, being pregnant and unmarried must have raised a few eyebrows."

Surprised by his change of topic, Maggie met his gaze.

"A few," she said warily.

"You haven't had an easy time of it, have you?" Dylan asked.

Seeing the compassion and understanding in his eyes, Maggie felt a lump of emotion lodge in her throat. She swallowed convulsively. "Waking up from a coma to discover you've lost your memory must have been a hundred times worse than anything I've had to deal with," she replied, hoping to steer the conversation in another direction.

Dylan held her gaze for a long moment before stepping aside.

Maggie bit back her sigh of relief. "How long were you in the coma?" she asked, determined now to keep the focus on Dylan and away from herself.

"Well…the accident happened back in October," Dylan said as he crossed to the French doors. "I was in a coma for four months…"

"October?" Maggie had been under the assumption his accident had happened only a few months ago.

"Yeah…around the fifteenth. I think that's what

they said,'' Dylan responded as he stood gazing out onto the deck.

Maggie couldn't move, couldn't breathe. October fifteenth was the day after her father and his aunt's funeral, the day after she and Dylan had made love, the day Dylan had driven back to San Diego.

Chapter Seven

Before Maggie could comment on Dylan's stunning revelation, a commotion in the hallway distracted her, and a few moments later Richard and Beverly Chason appeared in the kitchen doorway.

"Hi. I hope we're not interrupting." Beverly Chason's smile was tentative as her gaze darted between Maggie and Dylan.

Maggie responded with a smile of her own. "Of course not, Bev. Come on in. How was your day?" she asked politely, while her mind tried to assimilate the knowledge that Dylan's accident had to have happened the day he'd made the return trip to San Diego.

"We had a great day," Richard said. "We drove along the coast to Seaside and spent the morning watching the seabirds. After lunch we wandered around the stores and had dinner overlooking the water."

"Sounds wonderful. Can I interest you in a glass of iced tea?" Maggie asked.

"That would be lovely," Beverly responded. "Let me help you."

"No...really, I can manage," Maggie said. "Have a seat."

Dylan pulled out a chair for Beverly, and Richard sat down next to his wife. Maggie brought the jug of iced tea from the fridge and flashed Dylan a grateful smile when he set down four glasses.

"So...are you on holiday?" Richard's question was directed at Dylan.

"Darling," Bev interrupted. "Dylan is Maggie's business partner."

"That doesn't mean he isn't on holiday," Richard replied.

"He's actually on leave from the navy," Maggie piped up.

"Really," Richard said. "Oh, of course. You're Rosemary's nephew."

"That's right," Dylan replied.

"Thank you," Bev said, as Maggie slid a glass of iced tea toward her. "Richard and I were shocked and saddened when we read about Bill and Rosemary," Bev continued. "Such a tragedy...for you both."

"Thank you," Dylan said.

Maggie glanced over at Dylan as she filled the two remaining glasses.

"You know, I once gave serious thought to joining the navy," Richard said, and laughed at the astonished look on his wife's face. He reached over to cover her hand with his. "That was right after I lost track of you, my love."

"The navy? Richard, darling...you never told me that," Bev's surprise echoed through her voice.

"It was a fleeting notion at best," he quickly assured her as he glanced at Dylan leaning against the counter. "Where are you stationed?" he asked.

"Point Loma, San Diego," Dylan said, after a brief hesitation.

"That's the submarine base, isn't it?" Richard asked.

"Yes," Dylan replied, keeping his tone casual, all the while wondering how to redirect the conversation away from himself. A thought suddenly struck him. "Bev. You mentioned this morning that you and Richard met in Grace Harbor fifty years ago," Dylan said. "But Maggie told me there's more to the story."

"She's right," Bev acknowledged, flashing a tender smile at her husband.

"I've heard that story a hundred times," Richard said in a teasing voice. "I'm sure Dylan could tell a more exciting tale about the places he's seen."

"No...please," Dylan was quick to add. "I'd really like to hear it," he said with a smile.

Maggie felt her heart shudder in her breast in response to Dylan's smile, which she thought would have charmed the trunk off an elephant.

Bev's eyes glazed over and her cheeks turned a bright pink. "I was only sixteen when I met Richard," Bev began. "My family and I came to Grace Harbor for two weeks that summer...the best summer of my life."

"I was twenty-one," Richard said, jumping in, "and driving a beat-up jalopy to Phoenix, where my uncle had promised to help me find a job."

"Tired of the freeway, he'd followed the signs to Grace Harbor and stopped for a bite to eat," Bev picked up the tale. "He was walking on the sand—"

"Minding my own business," Richard chimed in.

"And I was running down the beach trying to get a kite to fly, when I ran right into him, knocking us both down," she explained. "It was all my fault," Beverly admitted, smiling at the memory. "But Richard apologized to me. Then he asked if he could buy me a soda."

"I knew right then and there she was the only girl for me," Richard said.

"We spent the afternoon together," Bev said. "Then he walked me back to the motel where I was staying with my parents. Richard wanted to meet them, but I knew they wouldn't approve, so I told him they were out."

"I couldn't leave," Richard explained. "So I found a cheap motel on the edge of town, and for the next two weeks we spent every moment we could together."

"I knew my folks would forbid me to see Richard, if they found out," Bev continued. "But by the end of the two weeks, Richard insisted on telling them. And so we did."

"That was my first mistake," Richard admitted with a sigh. "My second was letting her father talk me into agreeing not to see Beverly for six whole months. He said it would be a test of my love for her." Richard stopped and slowly shook his head.

"What I didn't realize," he went on, "was the lengths to which they were prepared to go to keep us apart." He reached over and squeezed his wife's hand. "Beverly and her parents lived in Seattle then, and though I was tempted to forget about Phoenix and my uncle, I needed the job. I didn't think six months was too long a time. Besides, her father told me I could write to her…and I did write, every day."

"I never got his letters," Beverly said. "My father never gave them to me. He destroyed them. My parents lied to us both, just to keep us apart." There was a sadness in her voice that tugged at Maggie's heart.

"Richard told me later that he'd tried to call me several times," Bev said, "but they fielded his calls and didn't pass on the messages he left."

"I went to Phoenix and got a job and kept telling myself everything would work out. When the six months were up I took some time off and drove to Seattle. But I was too late. They'd moved. I made some inquiries, but no one could tell me where they'd gone."

"My mother had worked on me, too, of course," Beverly said. "She told me holiday romances never lasted. Time went by, and I didn't hear from Richard, and I became convinced she was right, that he'd forgotten all about me. Three months later we moved to Dallas."

"So how did you meet each other again?" Dylan asked, his gaze intent, obviously caught up in the story.

"Do you believe in fate?" Richard asked, then smiled. "We do! Because it was fate that brought us back together," he stated. "Unfortunately for us, it took ten years."

"I threw myself into my studies and became a teacher." Beverly picked up the thread once more. "I tried to forget Richard, but I couldn't. I'm not sure what prompted me that summer, ten years later, to come back to Grace Harbor."

"I, on the other hand, had been coming back every summer, just in case," Richard unabashedly confessed.

"It's a wonderful story," Maggie said on a sigh. "Just like the plot from a romance novel. You are both so lucky to find each other again. True-life happy-ever-after tales are rare."

As she spoke, Maggie's gaze drifted to where Dylan sat across the table. His smile seemed wistful, and Maggie felt her heart trip over. For a split second she found herself wishing there could be a happy-ever-after ending for her, too.

It was a pipe dream, of course. Dylan didn't remember making love to her, didn't remember anything about the night they'd shared. And even if his memory returned, there was little hope for a future together as a family.

He was a career man through and through, a man who didn't believe in marriage, a man afraid to love and who kept his heart and his emotions hidden behind a thick protective wall.

"Enough about us," Richard was saying. "I'm curious to know why you joined the navy, Dylan."

Dylan's gaze flew to Maggie's, and she could see the look of panic that flashed into his eyes.

"To see the world," Maggie supplied. "Isn't that the reason most young men join up?" she joked.

Richard laughed. "From what I've heard, after you sign up, it's quite some time before you even see a ship. Is that true, Dylan?"

"For the most part," Dylan replied, though in truth he couldn't remember.

"I've always wanted to buy my own sailboat," Richard said, a wistful note in his voice. "But we're not anywhere near a lake or seaway, so there's little point."

"Oh...that reminds me," Maggie quickly jumped

in. "How much damage was done to your house? You mentioned you had to move out, didn't you?" she asked, diverting the conversation once more.

"Lightning struck a tree near the house, and a branch fell through the roof," Beverly said, quick to take the bait. "Luckily we weren't home at the time, but it did considerable damage."

"It was quite a mess," Richard said. "That's why we decided to renovate," he added, and proceeded to describe the extent of the renovations, together with the many run-ins they'd had with various tradespeople hired to do the work.

Maggie noted the relief in Dylan's eyes, and for the next half hour, conversation flowed.

A little later Maggie covered her mouth with her hand, trying unsuccessfully to stifle a yawn.

"Maggie, my dear. Why didn't you say you were tired," Beverly scolded gently. "How are you sleeping these days?"

"Fitfully," Maggie replied honestly. "Around nine at night I start to fade," she said, and as if to give truth to her words she yawned again. "Oh, dear. Excuse me."

Richard laughed. "We can take a hint," he teased. Pushing back his chair he rose from the table. "It's time we turned in, too. We have a big day ahead of us tomorrow. Good night."

"Good night, Maggie, Dylan. It's been lovely chatting with you," Beverly said as she followed her husband from the kitchen.

"Good night," Maggie and Dylan chorused.

"I'm bushed. I think I'll turn in, too," Dylan said. "Oh...by the way, I just wanted to say thanks."

"I'm sorry?" Maggie frowned.

"For managing to sidetrack the conversation away from me," Dylan explained.

"I imagine you get fed up having to explain to people about your loss of memory," Maggie said, warmed by his words.

"Since coming out of the coma, I haven't spoken to many people, other than the doctors and nurses who were treating me...oh, and my superior officers, of course," he said. "I've been keeping pretty much to myself. But from what I've been told, that isn't unusual for me.... I've always been a bit of a loner."

Maggie's heart twisted at the bleakness she could hear in his voice. She wished there was something she could say, but Dylan was already moving away.

"Good night," he said, and with a wave was gone.

Maggie added soap powder to the dishwasher and turned it on before making her way to her bedroom. A faint breeze wafted in through the open window, bringing with it the sweet scent of the roses from the flower bed outside.

With a tired sigh, Maggie undressed and crawled beneath the lightweight duvet cover. But sleep eluded her. Each time she closed her eyes, Dylan's familiar features would appear, the little-boy-lost look in his eyes.

What he'd said was true. He was a man who preferred to keep to himself, to stand on the sidelines and watch and listen.

Maggie remembered Rosemary telling her that she hadn't even known her sister was pregnant, hadn't known of Dylan's existence until she'd returned to the States after spending fifteen years living in Australia where she'd moved after she'd married a businessman from Melbourne.

When her husband died, Rosemary had returned to the States and tried to locate her younger sister. Friends and old neighbors had told her about her sister's child and the fact that she'd abandoned him. That's when Rosemary had taken it upon herself to track down her nephew.

It had proved to be a lengthy and time-consuming process, and when she'd finally found Dylan, he'd been thirteen-years-old.

According to Rosemary, he hadn't been interested in her or her invitation to come and live with her. She'd visited him every week trying to establish a bond, a connection, but he'd been rebellious and resentful, so filled with anger that she'd often despaired of getting through to him and forming any kind of relationship.

But over a period of a year when Rosemary had been tempted numerous times to throw in the towel, he'd finally agreed to live with her. He'd settled down and applied himself to his studies, but he'd still kept her at a distance, hiding behind a wall of resistance, afraid to let anyone close enough to hurt him.

On the evening of her father and Rosemary's funeral, after she and Dylan had returned to Fairwinds, Maggie had been surprised when Dylan had started talking so lovingly about his aunt.

He'd recounted several stories from their first weeks together, when he admitted he had tested her and pushed the boundaries as far as they would go, sure she'd grow tired of him and send him back to the foster home.

Listening to Dylan talk about his aunt that night, Maggie had seen a vulnerable and loving side to his personality, a side she'd never known existed.

The barrier had come down, at least for a while, and seeing the anguish and pain tearing at him, she'd fallen deeper under his spell. He'd even admitted he'd been wrong in thinking his aunt's marriage wouldn't last, adding that he'd never seen two people more in love and more suited to each other.

Tears stung Maggie's eyes and she bit back a sob, fearful Dylan would hear her and come and investigate, just as he'd done that night so long ago.

Stifling a moan, Maggie pushed the cover aside and eased herself into a sitting position. She took several deep breaths, deliberately trying to derail her thoughts from the path they were taking.

She gently massaged her stomach and smiled when the baby kicked her several times. With a sigh Maggie slid her legs off the bed and, pulling on her housecoat, headed for the baby's room.

Since entering the third trimester of her pregnancy, she'd found that the rocking chair was sometimes more conducive to sleep.

Setting the chair in motion, she closed her eyes, and almost instantly images of Dylan began to float into her mind. And so did the memory she'd been fighting since the moment he'd walked back into her life, the memory triggered by Bev and Richard's story, the memory of the night they'd made love.

Dylan had gone to bed. She had followed soon after. Feeling lost and lonely, devastated by the knowledge that she would never see her father or Rosemary again, she'd started to cry.

Tears had trickled down her face, and a sob had burst free as sorrow swamped her. Grabbing a tissue from the box on the bedside table and, fearful of waking Dylan, she'd buried her head in her pillow and wept uncontrollably.

A knock on her door, followed by Dylan's voice saying her name had brought a gasp from her lips, and she'd blown her nose, trying to compose herself.

"I'm all right," she'd whispered hoarsely as she'd fought to contain her sobs.

She had heard footsteps cross to her bed and felt his weight as he'd sat down next to her.

"Maggie, don't cry...you'll make yourself ill," Dylan had said softly, but the compassion and pain she could hear in his voice only made her cry harder.

"Please, just leave me," she said a few moments later, but her words were almost incoherent.

"Maggie..." Her name was a sigh on his lips, and when his arm went around her shoulders to lift her head from the pillow, she let out a whimper of protest. "I know exactly how you're feeling, Maggie, believe me," he said gently against her ear, his arms drawing her closer.

She hiccuped and blew her nose. "It's just not fair!" Her voice was a passionate whisper.

"You're right, it's not fair," he agreed evenly. "But in my experience life rarely ever is."

Maggie sniffed and drew away, realizing, with a startled gasp, that Dylan wasn't wearing a shirt, that he was naked from the waist up.

Her heart lurched painfully and a shiver of awareness raced through her. Dropping her gaze, she toyed with the wad of tissue in her hand.

"It's all right to cry, Maggie," Dylan was saying. "Crying is just part of the healing process. They were special people and we're going to miss them."

Hearing the anguish echoing in his voice, Maggie

raised her eyes to meet his. As their gazes collided her heart shuddered to a standstill, and the air between them was suddenly charged with tension, making it impossible for her to breathe.

They stared at each other for what seemed an eon but was little more than five seconds, until, like the opposite poles of a magnet, they closed the gap between them.

When his mouth touched hers, Maggie's heartbeat took off like a rocket. Sensation after sensation swamped her as he plundered and pillaged her mouth, drawing a response that thrilled and terrified her.

She'd been kissed before, but not like this...never like this. Desire burst to life deep inside her, sweeping like a wildfire through her to leave her body a quivering mass of need.

She drew a ragged breath, inhaling the smell of the ocean and a deeper richer masculine scent that was Dylan.

Suddenly Dylan broke the kiss, holding her at arm's length. She could feel his muscles tremble with the effort, and she felt herself sway toward him when she saw, reflected in his eyes, the same desire running rampant inside her.

"Maggie," he said huskily. "We have to stop..."

Maggie felt as if he'd slapped her. "You don't want me?" She forced the words past trembling lips, tears stinging her eyes once more.

"Oh, I want you. Make no mistake about that," Dylan muttered through clenched teeth, his hands tightening on her arms. "But we can't—surely you understand, this is insane."

But Maggie covered his mouth with her fingers, cutting off further protests, and when she felt the tremor that ran through him her heart soared. The knowledge that he wanted her fed her growing need for him, and with a boldness she hadn't known she possessed she leaned forward to place her mouth on his.

The kiss was as tentative as it was reckless, and for half a heartbeat Dylan kept himself rigid, then the dam burst and he was kissing her as if there was no tomorrow.

Maggie responded with all the love that was in her heart, and when his hands deftly discarded her nightdress and began to feverishly explore the contours of her body, she gasped in wonder at the sensations spiraling through her.

That he was a highly accomplished lover was soon made evident by the way he aroused her with long, deep kisses that rekindled the fire within her and made her burn with unbridled desire. His tender hands teased her until she was writhing in frustration, moving ever closer to the edge of reason.

Following his lead, she explored his body with an eagerness that almost made her blush, stroking the firm muscles of his back, skimming over the smattering of hairs on his broad chest and caressing his firm buttocks. Her reward was hearing the low growls of pleasure from deep in his throat and the thunderous roar of his heart.

And just when she thought she'd already reached the heavens, he gently slid inside her to take her on that final, incredible journey to a magical place beyond the stars.

Exhausted, they'd lain in each other's arms, floating in the euphoria of the aftermath of their lovemaking. When her heartbeat had returned to normal, she'd opened her eyes to see Dylan gazing at her with a look she hadn't quite been able to decipher.

He'd reached for her again, and she'd gone into his arms willingly, holding tightly to a thin thread of hope that what they'd shared would be the beginning of a long and lasting relationship.

But that was then. Tears slowly seeped from beneath her lashes to trace a path down her cheek.

"Maggie? Why are you sitting here? Is everything all right?" The sound of Dylan's voice brought her eyes wide open and sent her heart into a tailspin. Hurriedly she brushed the tears away, glad of the shadows that helped to hide her face.

"I'm fine," she managed to say, though her voice wavered slightly. "I was uncomfortable and couldn't sleep, that's all." With some effort she rose from the rocking chair and pulled her housecoat around her.

"I couldn't sleep, either," he told her, then stopped. "You've been crying," he said, obviously catching the glint of wetness on her eyelashes as he approached. "Are you sure you're all right?" he repeated.

Maggie hesitated but only for a second. Before he could probe further, she moved past him, coming to a halt in the doorway.

"Sleeplessness is a side effect of being eight months pregnant," she stated evenly.

"What about crying, is that a side effect, too?" he asked, his voice almost a whisper. She didn't answer him but headed down the hall to her room.

Dylan stood for a long moment staring after her, feeling strangely bereft. He moved to the rocking chair and lowered himself into it, aware all the while of the lingering scent of the woman who'd recently been its occupant.

Maggie had looked as if she was carrying the world on her shoulders, and as he gazed into the darkness he found himself wishing there was some way he could ease her burden.

Chapter Eight

Maggie woke with a start. She glanced at the radio alarm on her bedside table and saw that it was almost eight thirty. She'd slept in.

With a groan she pushed the duvet cover aside and rolled out of bed. Ten minutes later, dressed in a blue maternity blouse and white pedal pushers, her hair tied back in a loose ponytail, she hurried down the hallway.

The distinct aroma of coffee assailed her as she reached the kitchen, and Maggie was relieved Beverly had taken it upon herself to make herself at home.

"Bev, I'm so sor—" she began, but the words died in her throat when she saw Dylan standing at the sink.

"Good morning." Dylan greeted her, flashing a smile.

Maggie felt a shiver pass up from her toes in response to his smile. She darted a quick glance around the kitchen, noting the table was set for one.

"Uh...good morning," she replied, frowning now.

"Have a seat," Dylan invited. "Coffee's ready, and there's a glass of juice for you on the table." He reached for the carafe of coffee. "Did you have a good night's rest?" he asked, following her toward the table.

"Yes. Oh...thank you," she murmured as he pulled out the chair for her. "This is very nice, Dylan, but I really should make breakfast for the Chasons. I'm afraid I overslept. They're probably wondering if I've forgotten about them."

"They've already eaten," Dylan calmly informed her as he filled the coffee cup in front of her.

Maggie threw him a startled look. "What? But...why didn't you wake me?"

"Last night you said you have trouble sleeping," he countered. "When you weren't in the kitchen this morning, I thought it best not to disturb you. Beverly agreed."

"But what—"

"About their breakfast?" he finished for her. "That was simple enough. You keep the fridge well stocked. I used eggs, cheese and mushrooms and made an omelette. Would you like one?"

"You cooked an omelette?" she asked, unable to hide her surprise.

"It's quite easy," he said, his eyes twinkling with humor. "I'd be happy to give you a demonstration of my culinary skills," he added, a smile tugging at the corner of his mouth.

"Sure...by all means," she said.

"No morning sickness today?" he asked as he retrieved a carton of eggs from the fridge.

"No," she replied. "I think it must have been the bacon that set me off yesterday." She watched him break first one egg then another into the bowl on the counter. "Are Richard and Bev still here?" she asked.

"They left ten minutes ago," Dylan said easily as he began to whisk the eggs with a fork. "Toast?" he asked.

"Yes, please," she said, warmed by his thoughtfulness. She couldn't remember the last time someone had cooked for her. "Did they say where they were heading?" Maggie asked, taking a sip of orange juice.

"Mount Saint Helens," he replied as he carried the bowl to the stove.

Maggie watched as he dropped a pat of butter into the frying pan and waited for it to melt before he poured in the egg mixture.

A few minutes later Dylan set a plate with an omelette and two slices of toast in front of her.

Maggie smiled up at him. "Thanks. It looks wonderful." She reached for her fork. "But what about you? Aren't you having any?"

"I ate earlier," he assured her. Crossing to the counter he refilled his coffee cup. "I'll leave you to it and get to work on those stairs," he said. "Yell if you need anything."

"I'll be fine," Maggie said, managing to hide her disappointment, annoyed with herself for wishing he would stay and keep her company.

The omelette was delicious, and as Maggie pushed the plate aside and lingered over a second glass of juice, she knew she could easily grow accustomed to being spoiled in this manner, especially if Dylan was the one doing the spoiling.

For the remainder of the week Maggie made a point of setting her alarm each morning in order to

make breakfast for the Chasons and Dylan. After
Richard and Beverly set out on their daily excursion,
Dylan would refill his coffee cup then head outside
to continue work on the stairs.

At midday Maggie would bring Dylan a lunch tray
and leave it on the picnic table. Then she'd wander
across the lawn to the small vegetable garden, stoop-
ing awkwardly now and then to pull out a weed.

The warm sunny weather prevailed, but Maggie
found that in her advanced state of pregnancy, her
energy soon waned and she had to return to the house
to rest.

Each afternoon as she prepared their evening meal,
she wondered how long Dylan planned to stay on at
Grace Harbor. She silently admitted to herself that she
was glad of his presence and was coming to rely on
him.

At times she would find herself drifting off into a
fantasy, dreaming that she and Dylan were a married
couple joyfully awaiting the birth of their first child.

By the end of the week Dylan's work on the stairs
was all but complete. Maggie had noticed that with
each passing day, the physical work he was doing
seemed to diminish the tension in him, making him
more at ease.

She'd also become increasingly aware of the fact
that under the sun's warm rays, Dylan's long, lean
body was slowly turning a deep bronze, and his muscles were toning up as his strength and stamina returned.

For Maggie, getting a good night's sleep continued
to be a problem. She lay staring at the ceiling, unable

to find a comfortable position. Her back ached, and the baby was restless.

Not for the first time, Maggie wondered if somehow the child sensed the tension building inside her—a tension that had more to do with Dylan's presence than with her approaching due date.

Maggie eased the duvet aside and swung her legs onto the floor. Waddling over to the window, she gazed up at the star-studded sky, gently massaging her lower back in an attempt to relieve the dull ache.

Two or three times during her pregnancy she'd had a strong craving for ice cream and pickles, and suddenly a longing for the cool icy taste of strawberries combined with the tang of a dill pickle tugged at her.

Her mouth began to water in anticipation, and the baby kicked her repeatedly as if in encouragement. Pulling on her housecoat, she slid her feet into her slippers and tiptoed from her room.

Not bothering to turn on any lights, she padded to the kitchen, and in the light cast by the moon she glanced at the numbers on the microwave oven, noting it was almost three in the morning.

"Ouch..." she grunted softly when she accidentally stubbed her toe on one of the kitchen chairs. Tears sprang into her eyes, but she blinked them away.

Mumbling under her breath, she hobbled to the refrigerator. The freezer was full of the extra meals she'd been cooking and storing there, meals that would help her through the first weeks after the baby was born when she knew she wouldn't feel like cooking.

Scanning the frozen packages, she saw no sign of

the small tub of ice cream she'd bought for just such
an occasion.

Her toe was throbbing and her fingers were numb
with cold as she rummaged through various items.
When her eyes lit on the tub of strawberry ice cream
nestled under the ice cube tray, she smiled in triumph.

Lifting the ice cube tray, she tried to liberate the
tub of ice cream, but her fingers were so cold she
couldn't get a good grip.

"Need any help?"

At the sound of Dylan's voice, Maggie let out a
squeal. Her half-frozen fingers lost what little hold
they had, and the ice cube tray slid from her grasp
and crashed to the floor.

"Ouch! Oh…!" Maggie moaned as cold ice cubes
bounced off her feet and scattered across the kitchen
floor.

"Maggie! I'm sorry," Dylan quickly came to her
aid, catching the tub of ice cream before it fell.

Dylan closed the freezer door and turned to Maggie. "I didn't mean to startle you," he said. "What
were you looking for?" he asked.

To his astonishment Maggie burst into tears.

"My God! Maggie, are you hurt?" he asked, fearful she'd somehow injured herself. Maggie shook her
head, continuing to cry.

"Aw…don't." Dylan chided softly. Putting his
arms around her, he drew her against him, silently
berating himself for making her cry.

Her hair felt like silk against his cheek, and her
skin smelled like freshly squeezed lemons. Dylan
continued to gently rock her, waiting for the tears to
subside. Her swollen abdomen was nestled firmly

against him, and for a brief moment he felt the baby move.

His breath caught in his throat at the fleeting sensation and, not for the first time, wondered what he should do about the strange and bizarre situation he'd found himself in.

Throughout the past week, he'd thrown himself into the physical activity of tearing down and rebuilding the stairs. The act of building something with his hands had somehow helped restore not only his strength but his self-confidence. And along with that came a renewed sense of peace and contentment, feelings that surprised and frightened him.

He knew he'd been deliberately avoiding the issue facing him and the decisions he would soon have to make regarding Maggie and...his child.

He hadn't gotten around to asking Maggie questions about their relationship, about the plans—if any—they'd made together. Each time he'd thought about bringing up the subject, he hadn't been able to find the right words.

And as for Maggie. She'd quietly gone about her business, making no demands on him with regard to the baby, or pressuring him into trying to remember the past.

She'd given him breathing space to come to terms with the curveballs he'd been thrown, and he admired her for that and her strong, independent spirit.

Dylan drew a deep breath, drawing in the sweet scent of her deep into his lungs. Holding Maggie in his arms could easily become addictive, he thought, and instantly felt the faint stirrings of desire.

Shock ricocheted through him and suddenly, like a

bolt out of the blue, he was visited with a strong impression that he'd held Maggie in his arms like this before…that he'd kissed her…before.

Dylan's heart shuddered to a halt and he pulled away to hold Maggie at arm's length. She gazed up at him her eyes awash with tears.

What would happen if he kissed her now? Would he remember?

"Oh-h-h," Maggie groaned, and Dylan watched as her face twisted in a look of surprise.

"Maggie? What is it? What's wrong?" he asked, his tone urgent. "Is it the baby?"

"I don't know…I think so… It feels so strange," Maggie said. Her fingers gripped his arm.

Dylan fought to remain calm. He tightened his hold on her and helped her to the nearest chair. Once she was seated, he reached for the telephone and punched in the emergency numbers.

Heart racing, he answered the operator's questions, giving the address without a second thought, his gaze all the while on Maggie.

"An ambulance will be here in a few minutes," he told her when he hung up, and at his words she managed a weak smile. "I'll unlock the front door," he said.

"Okay," Maggie said as the uncomfortable sensation of her skin growing taut across her abdomen began again.

Was it a contraction? She couldn't be sure, but something was definitely happening. At the prenatal classes she'd attended, the instructor had tried to cover any eventuality, to help alleviate some of the worry of giving birth.

Dr. Whitney had encouraged her to sign up for the

classes, even suggesting she ask someone to accompany her and act as coach during her labor. But having no family to turn to and no close friend to call upon, she'd gone to the classes on her own.

There had been five women in the class, each in the late stages of pregnancy. At first Maggie had been embarrassed by the fact that she was the only unmarried mother-to-be, but for the baby's sake she'd put on a smile and joined in the sessions.

"I hear a siren," Dylan said, cutting into Maggie's thoughts. "How are you feeling?" he asked.

"I don't know...I'm not sure if I'm in labor...I'm getting these weird sensations," she tried to explain.

"We'll let the medics decide," Dylan said before heading off to greet the emergency team.

"She's in the kitchen," Maggie heard Dylan say, and seconds later two attendants appeared wheeling a stretcher.

"Is this your first baby?" one of the attendants asked.

"Yes."

"When are you due?" The question came from the second man.

"In about two weeks," Maggie answered.

"Tell me what happened," the attendant said, pulling out his stethoscope.

"I got up to get...a drink," she began. "And suddenly I felt a pressure and a tightening across my abdomen...it startled me—" She faltered.

The attendant didn't respond, he was listening to the sounds coming through his stethoscope.

"The baby's heartbeat is strong," he told her when he glanced up. "Everything seems all right. But, just to be on the safe side, I think you should come to the hospital and get a thorough checkup.''

"Good idea." Dylan was quick to support the decision. "I'll follow in my car."

Maggie was too tired to resist. Over the attendant's shoulder, she could see Beverly and Richard Chason in their dressing gowns, anxious expressions on their faces.

"Is there anything we can do?" Beverly asked, inching forward.

Maggie smiled. "Nothing, thanks."

"Perhaps we should leave in the morning," Richard suggested.

"Oh...please don't go." Maggie's voice held concern. "I'd hate to think I've chased my favorite customers away."

"We're thinking of you, my dear," Beverly said. "Having us here is extra work for you."

"Don't be silly," Maggie assured them. "Please stay."

"Of course we will," Richard said, before stepping out of the way of the attendant.

Throughout the ride to the hospital, Maggie found her thoughts returning to those moments in the kitchen just before the strange spasm had enveloped her. Having Dylan's arms around her and hearing the murmur of his voice in her ear had made her feel warm and safe and...loved.

She wished...oh, how she wished— Maggie closed her eyes, quickly clamping down on the foolish notion and telling herself she might as well be wishing for the moon.

Dylan applied pressure to the brakes and watched the red taillights of the ambulance turn into the hospital's emergency entrance.

He pulled into the parking lot and hurriedly made his way into the five-story building.

Once inside he followed the color-coded lines painted on the floor and soon found the emergency area, but he could see no sign of Maggie or the ambulance attendants.

Dylan approached the nurse's desk. "Excuse me, I'm looking for Maggie Fairchild," he said. "She was brought in by ambulance a few minutes ago."

The nurse glanced at the pile of charts in front of her. Behind her stood a set of automatic doors, but its windows were made of opaque protective glass making it impossible for Dylan to see anything or anyone.

"Doctor Taylor is with her now," the nurse informed him. "There's a waiting area right over there," she said, pointing to the alcove where several people were already seated.

"Thank you." Dylan ignored her suggestion and retraced his steps along the corridor, coming to a halt at the door leading outside.

Too restless to sit and wait, he paced the length of the hallway again. After his own prolonged stay at the hospital in San Diego, he'd developed a strong aversion for them.

On his fourth sojourn down the corridor, two nurses passed him, each flashed a friendly smile in his direction, but he hardly noticed them, his mind preoccupied with thoughts of Maggie.

When Dylan approached the waiting area once more, the emergency doors swung open, and a man wearing a white coat emerged.

"Dr. Taylor! Could you sign this release?" The question came from the nurse at the desk, and Dylan watched as the man returned to do as she asked.

"Thank you, Doctor," said the nurse.

The man nodded, then strode toward Dylan.

"Dr. Taylor?" Dylan said as the doctor drew abreast of him.

The doctor slowed to a halt. "Yes," he responded.

"The nurse told me you were examining...Maggie Fairchild..." Dylan began. "Is she...?

"Ah...Mr. Fairchild?" The doctor smiled and extended his hand in a firm handshake. "Your wife is Dr. Whitney's patient. And let me assure you she's doing fine," the doctor said.

"Is she...? I mean she's not in labor—" Dylan broke off, ignoring the doctor's mistaken assumption that he was Maggie's husband.

"No...she's not in labor," the doctor was quick to confirm, his expression serious. "I'm pretty sure what she's experiencing are what's known as Braxton-Hicks contractions. They usually last about thirty seconds and aren't too painful. It's just the uterus practicing for the real event," he explained.

"Oh...I see...." Dylan was relieved to hear neither Maggie nor the baby were in any danger.

"You can take your wife home," he said. "And I'd suggest that for the next few days you pamper her a little," he added with a smile.

"I'll do that. Thank you," Dylan replied.

Dr. Taylor nodded, then moved on. Dylan stood for a moment watching the doctor leave. Suddenly the sound of voices reached him, and he turned to see two nurses striding down the corridor toward him. As they passed, he caught a snippet of their conversation.

"You have to admire her," said the nurse nearest to Dylan.

"Any guesses on who the baby's father is?" the second nurse asked.

"Maggie certainly isn't saying," the first nurse replied. "And she's going to keep the baby...these days that takes guts."

As the voices faded, Dylan stood rooted to the spot, realizing with a jolt that they'd been talking about his Maggie, and it was obvious Maggie's condition and the identity of the baby's father was still a source of gossip in town.

No wonder Maggie kept to herself, he mused. Dylan slowly retraced his steps to the nurse's desk.

"Dr. Taylor told me I can take Maggie Fairchild home," he told the nurse.

The nurse smiled. "Yes. It was a false alarm. I'll get a nurse to bring her out," she went on. "Oh...here she is now."

When Maggie caught sight of Dylan's tall familiar figure standing at the nurse's desk, her heart gave a little leap of joy.

While the doctor and nurses had been kind and solicitous throughout the ordeal, she was exhausted, and simply wanted to go home and crawl into bed.

"You can bring your car around to the emergency entrance, if it's easier," the nurse suggested.

"Great. Thanks," Dylan said. "I'll be right back," he added, flashing Maggie a smile.

Throughout the ride back to Fairwinds, Dylan seemed preoccupied, but Maggie found the silence soothing.

"You must be tired," Dylan said as he made the turn onto Indigo Street.

"Somehow I don't think I'll have any trouble sleeping now," she replied with a sigh.

"This hasn't been easy for you has it?" Dylan said.

Maggie looked over at him, but in the dim lighting of the car's interior she could barely see his profile. "I'm not sure I understand. If you're talking about my pregnancy, then it's been fairly straightforward, apart from occasional bouts of morning sickness."

"You're still a source of gossip in town, did you know that?" he asked.

"Of course," she responded easily, pretending a nonchalance that at times during the past eight-and-a-half months, she'd been hard-pressed to maintain.

"Doesn't it bother you?" Dylan asked, pulling the car into the driveway.

"Only if I let it," she said abruptly. "The truth is, I'm an unmarried woman who is having a baby, and while the rest of the world might not care, in a small community like Grace Harbor, I'd be a fool if I thought everyone in town would applaud or approve of my situation."

"What if you were married?" Dylan asked as he shut off the car's engine.

"I'm sorry? What did you say?" Maggie asked.

Dylan turned to look at her. "I said, what if you were married?" he repeated.

Maggie's heart lurched inside her breast. There was something about the tone of Dylan's voice...something in his eyes that sent a shiver skidding down her spine.

"But I'm not," she managed to say.

"Then I think we should remedy that as soon as possible." Dylan said. "I think we should get married."

Chapter Nine

"Wha—what did you say?" Maggie's voice was little more than a whisper. She had to be dreaming. It was the only explanation.

"I said, I think we should get married," Dylan answered, but before he could say more, two figures appeared, one on each side of the car.

Dylan opened the driver's side door and climbed out. "Is everything all right?" Richard asked, leaning in to look at Maggie.

Maggie nodded as her door opened.

"We were beginning to think you must have gone into labor after all," Beverly said, gazing anxiously at Maggie.

"No. The doctor said I was having Braxton-Hicks contractions. False labor, I guess. Everything is fine," Maggie said before releasing her seat belt and easing out of the car.

"You poor dear, you must be frozen and exhausted." Beverly put her arm around Maggie.

"Would you like me to make you a cup of tea, or perhaps you'd prefer a glass of warm milk?"

"Thanks Bev, but I just want to climb into bed and get some sleep. It was very sweet of you both to wait up. I'm only sorry I disturbed your night's rest." She gave the older woman's arm a squeeze.

"Don't be silly," Bev chastised, patting Maggie's hand as they went inside. "And if there's anything we can do for you, you only have to ask."

Maggie slowed to a halt when she reached the hall leading to her bedroom. "Thanks Bev. Uh...about breakfast tomorrow—"

"Maggie, please!" Beverly was quick to cut in. "Don't give it a thought. We'll manage."

"I'll take care of breakfast," Dylan said as he and Richard joined them.

Maggie threw him a grateful glance. "Thank you. And thanks for coming to the hospital with me."

"No problem," Dylan replied easily.

"I'll say good-night, then."

"Good night, my dear." Beverly leaned over and kissed Maggie's cheek.

Blinking back tears, Maggie headed down the hall to her bedroom. As she crawled into bed, she glanced at the clock, surprised to see it was almost five.

Only two hours had passed since she'd headed to the kitchen in search of a dish of ice cream and pickles, but a lot had happened in that short space of time. Though the strange sensations she'd experienced had frightened her at first, she knew if Dylan hadn't been there to prevent a fall, the results might well have been more drastic.

But uppermost in her mind was Dylan's startling

proposal of marriage. Had he really proposed? Maggie shook her head. Surely not!

Maggie closed her eyes and tried to re-create those moments outside the house, but her brain refused to cooperate, and slowly she drifted off to sleep.

Maggie stretched her arms above her head and let out a sigh of contentment, reluctant to open her eyes and let the day in.

She felt the baby move and stretch, as if he, too, was waking up, and with loving hands she gently massaged her abdomen, smiling when she received a kick in response.

Opening her eyes, Maggie glanced at the clock radio, not at all surprised to see it was already past ten. But she refused to feel guilty about sleeping in, not after the previous evening's events, and knowing that in a few short weeks she'd have a newborn baby to take care of and wouldn't be able to enjoy the simple luxury of staying in bed.

Suddenly her peace was shattered by a loud knock. Before she could respond, the door opened and Dylan walked in carrying a breakfast tray.

"Good morning," he said cheerily. "I thought you might enjoy breakfast in bed," he added as he approached the bed.

"Dylan...that's very kind of you," Maggie murmured, moved immeasurably by his kind gesture. Clutching the covers she watched him set the tray on the foot of her bed.

"You've lost a pillow." Bending down he retrieved it. "Shall I prop it behind you?" he asked, flashing her one of his irresistible smiles.

"Yes, thank you," Maggie managed to say as she struggled into a sitting position.

As Dylan leaned toward her to place the pillow behind her head, his clean, masculine scent swirled around her, catapulting her pulse into overdrive.

An ache blossomed in her breast, and her breath locked in her throat in reaction to his nearness. All at once she was bombarded with memories of the night he'd held her in his arms while she cried, the night he'd kissed her and set her soul on fire, the night they'd shared a passion she knew she'd never forget.

Maggie clenched her fingers around the duvet cover to prevent herself from reaching up and throwing her arms around his neck. She could feel his warm breath tickle her forehead, and the yearning to be held in his arms again almost overwhelmed her.

Dylan withdrew and lifted the tray closer to Maggie, noticing as he did how incredibly sexy she looked with her hair tousled from sleep, her cheeks a delicate shade of pink, her mouth full and inviting.

For a fleeting moment his gaze locked with hers, and in the depths of her brown eyes he saw an emotion he didn't recognize, an emotion he couldn't quite decipher.

"I hope you like pancakes," he said before moving to the window.

"They're my favorite," she told him.

Dylan stood gazing out at the cloud-filled sky.

"The weather forecast calls for showers today," he commented.

"The garden could use a good watering," Maggie responded, relieved her voice sounded normal, still trying to ride out the wave of need his nearness had evoked. She reached for the glass of orange juice on the tray.

Dylan turned from the window and slowly let his gaze travel around Maggie's bedroom. That she loved flowers was obvious from the way her room was decorated. Wallpaper depicting baskets overflowing with pink and red fuchsias highlighted one wall, and a number of framed pictures with a floral theme were hanging around the room.

His gaze drifted to the antique triple-mirrored dressing table on the wall opposite the bed. In the mirrors he could see three reflections of Maggie as she reclined against the pillows.

Suddenly a prickling sensation danced down his spine. The feeling that he'd stood in this exact spot before, gazing at Maggie asleep on the bed, gripped him.

His heart shuddered to a halt, and pain exploded behind his eyes as an assortment of fragmented images flashed inside his head.

Dylan closed his eyes, trying desperately to focus on just one image. And then it happened...the flashing pictures slowed to blend into one clear and startling image. Maggie, with her hair spread across the pillow...Maggie, lying naked on her bed, Maggie, her eyes ablaze with passion.

As quickly as the evocative image appeared it vanished, and a moan of protest burst free before he could contain it.

"Dylan, what's wrong?" The urgency in Maggie's voice cut through his mental haze and he met her gaze, seeing the concern for him in her eyes.

"Nothing...it's nothing...just a muscle spasm. I

get them sometimes,'' he lied, wanting simply to dispel her anxiety.

Tempted as he was to tell her the truth, he silently rationalized that rather than a memory, the images he'd seen might well have been a manifestation of the desire he'd begun to secretly harbor for Maggie.

"Did the doctors give you any medication?'' she asked, guessing from the way Dylan's glance slid away from hers, that he wasn't telling the truth.

"No, but I'll be fine,'' he told her as he walked to the door. "Enjoy your breakfast,'' he said. "There's no hurry. Richard and Bev have gone for the day, and if you need me, I'll be outside putting sealer on the stairs before the rain starts.''

Alone once more, Maggie sank back against the pillows, her appetite gone. Something had happened to Dylan a few moments ago, she was sure of it. Had his memory returned?

The urge to go after him and ask was strong, but Maggie made no move toward the door, torn between wanting to know what had caused his reaction and a desire to have him trust her enough to tell her on his own.

After a refreshing shower, Maggie dressed in a bright blue maternity blouse and cream-colored slacks. Twisting her hair into a knot at the base of her neck, she made her way to the kitchen.

A quick glance outside revealed Dylan standing at the foot of the stairs, a paintbrush in his hands. Not for the first time, Maggie admitted to herself that he'd done as good a job building the new stairs as any skilled carpenter.

After clearing away the items from her breakfast tray, she wandered down the hall to the baby's room.

She came to a halt in the doorway and stared in stunned surprise when she saw the crib standing against the far wall.

Tears stung her eyes, and a tingling warmth spread through her. Dylan must have assembled the crib while she was sleeping. Her throat closed over with emotion, and a tear spilled down her cheek as she crossed to stand at the crib.

He'd surprised her again with his thoughtfulness, and suddenly she found herself remembering how angry and frustrated Dylan had been by the loss of his memory. During the past week as he'd worked on the stairs, he'd seemed more at peace with himself, more content than the Dylan she'd known.

Could the accident be responsible for the change in him? she wondered. Horrifying as it must have been to wake and realize all his memories were lost, it appeared a new Dylan had emerged, a Dylan without the protective wall he used to have around himself.

This Dylan was more open and giving, tender and thoughtful, compassionate and caring, the same qualities he'd revealed to her on the night they'd made love.

She'd revelled in his passion, his warmth. But in the cold light of day she'd watched him revert back to the disciplined officer, the man in control. Like a groundhog when he glimpses his shadow, Dylan had scrambled back into his cave, leaving her to wonder if she'd ever see him again.

With a sigh, Maggie turned to the rocking chair. She sat down and slowly ran her hands over her abdomen.

"You gave me quite a scare last night," she spoke

softly to the baby, drawing comfort from her own voice. "I thought for a minute you'd decided to make an early appearance," she added, and in response felt a nudge from an elbow.

She smiled. "Yes...I know," she continued in the same soft tone, acknowledging the baby's movements. "But I guess you weren't ready to face the world, at least not yet. I can't say I blame you...I'm not ready, either...to be a mother, that is."

Maggie was silent for a long moment, and as if to offer her encouragement, the baby kicked her gently several times.

"It's just that being a parent is such a tremendous responsibility. Sometimes I get scared—and wonder if I'll be any good at it." Maggie sighed.

This time the baby responded by jabbing her sharply. "Well! Does that mean you're worried, too?" She chuckled softly, believing with all her heart that her unborn child understood exactly what she was saying.

"I do love you," she whispered, massaging her abdomen once more. "We'll just have to learn together, won't we? You and I," she said.

"Oh—ouch!" Maggie reacted to the hard kick that landed close to one of her kidneys. "Hey, take it easy, will you?" she protested.

"Okay...what do you think? Was I dreaming last night or did your father propose? I know he's just being kind, trying to do the right thing." She sighed again.

"He doesn't even remember me, and besides—" she hurried on, not sure who she was trying to convince "—when two people get married, they should be in love with each other, deeply in love. Dylan doesn't love me—'' Her voice cracked as sadness tightened in her throat.

The ring of the telephone cut through her mutterings. Maggie rose from the rocking chair and headed to the kitchen, ignoring the little voice inside her head that kept insisting every baby needed and deserved the love and support a father could provide.

"Hello?" Maggie said.

"Maggie? It's Elaine from Dr. Whitney's office," said the caller.

"Hi, Elaine," Maggie responded.

"Dr. Whitney just heard you paid a brief visit to the hospital last night," Elaine said. "He wanted me to call and ask if you'd like to come in a little earlier this afternoon. Is that a problem?"

"No," Maggie said. "What time?"

"Is two o'clock all right?" Elaine asked.

"Sure. I'll see you then," Maggie assured her.

Hungry, Maggie made up a plate of cheese and tomato sandwiches. Opening the French doors, she stepped onto the deck and across to the top of the stairs.

Dylan was kneeling on the cement below putting the finishing touches to the bottom step.

"Dylan, lunch is ready," she called down.

He glanced up and smiled. "Great. I'll clean the brush and be with you in a jiffy."

"The stairs look terrific," Maggie said. "You've done a good job."

"Thanks," Dylan replied. "It's nice to know there's something I'm good at. Let's hope my new-found talent can be applied to the roof."

Maggie smiled and nodded, surprised at the relief she felt on learning that his stay would be extended at least as long as it took to put a new roof on the house.

She returned to the kitchen and sat down at the table, absently reaching for a sweet pickle from the dish she'd set out.

Dylan appeared a few minutes later, and after washing his hands at the sink, he joined her. "I'm starving," he said as he sat down opposite Maggie and reached for a sandwich.

"Help yourself to a pickle," Maggie said.

Dylan glanced at the pickle dish then back at Maggie. "I would," he said. "But there doesn't appear to be any."

"What?" Maggie glanced at the dish that had been full a few minutes ago. "I must have eaten them all," she said, and felt her cheeks grow warm with embarrassment.

Dylan's low rumble of laughter sent a shiver of longing through her. "I guess you did," he said, his eyes alight with humor.

"I'll get more."

"Forget it," he replied easily.

They ate in silence for several minutes.

"Oh...I wanted to thank you for putting the crib together," Maggie said, darting a quick glance at him. "I'm hopeless at assembling things. Was it difficult?"

"No. Easier than building the stairs," Dylan said, his voice laced with amusement.

Maggie smiled. "You obviously have a talent for building things," she said, and felt her breath catch in her throat when his mouth curved into a heart-stopping smile.

"I certainly enjoy working with my hands." He

reached for the glass of milk on the table, his long, tanned fingers curling around the glass. He lifted it to his mouth and drank the remainder down. "Have you thought about what I said?" he suddenly asked.

Maggie felt her heart skip a beat. "About what?"

"About us getting married," he replied evenly.

"Oh...that." Maggie tried to keep her tone light and breezy. "I didn't think you were serious," she said, and noticed the tightening of his jaw at her response.

"Of course I'm serious," he said. "As the baby's father, I feel an obligation to do what's right for both you and the child."

Maggie made no reply, torn between a yearning to say yes and a need to tell Dylan the truth about their relationship.

"I'm curious," Dylan went on. "I get the impression we hadn't made plans to get married. You're not wearing a ring, so I assume we weren't engaged. So tell me, what kind of relationship did we have?" he asked.

Maggie drew a deep breath and met his steady gaze. "No, we hadn't made plans to marry," she confirmed, wondering at the pain slicing through her. "As to our relationship...well, you see, it wasn't at all what you think—" She stopped to a halt. "This isn't easy."

"Do you think it's easy for me?" Dylan demanded, his eyes shimmering with frustration. "At least you know. You remember," he went on. "Do you have any idea what it's been like for me?"

Maggie heard the torment in his voice, and her heart ached anew for him, for what he'd been through...was still going through.

"We were lovers for one night," she blurted out and saw shock register in his eyes. She looked down at the table. "You'd driven up from San Diego for the funeral. You had to leave the next morning. It was late, we'd both gone to bed. I was too upset to sleep. I starting crying. I couldn't seem to stop crying. You heard me and came into my bedroom—" She stopped, her throat burning with emotion.

Maggie kept her gaze focused on her hands clasped tightly together in front of her, like white ropes entwined. The silence was deafening. She drew a ragged breath, determined to finish what she'd started.

"We were both in a highly emotional state that night.... You were trying to comfort me...we were comforting each other—" She broke off. The silence stretched for what seemed an eternity.

Blinking back tears, Maggie raised her eyes to meet Dylan's, expecting to see a look of anger, perhaps even distaste in their gray depths, but to her astonishment there was only compassion and understanding.

Relief, sharp and real, spread through her. She swallowed convulsively. "So you shouldn't feel any obligation..." Her voice trailed off.

"That doesn't change the fact that I'm the baby's father," Dylan calmly pointed out. "Thank you. I admire you for your honesty, Maggie, for telling me the truth about what happened between us," he said, his tone sincere. "But I still think we should get married. It's the right thing to do, at least for the baby's sake."

Maggie stared in disbelief. After what she'd just told him, he still thought they should get married?

For a fleeting moment a feeling of joy swept through her, but she quickly quashed it, realizing Dylan was merely trying to do the honorable thing. And while she applauded his noble gesture, she reminded herself that when his memory returned and he remembered his true feelings about marriage, he would quickly regret his impulsive action and ask for his freedom.

He'd broken her heart once already, and she wasn't about to hand it over for a second go-round. Besides, she had the baby's welfare to think about.

"I don't think it would be—" Maggie started to say, but before she could finish, the telephone rang. Rising from the chair, she went to the phone.

"Hello!"

"Maggie, it's Jared! I'm sorry I haven't been by to see you. How are you?"

"I'm fine," Maggie replied.

"Is your new business partner still around?" he asked.

"Yes, he's right here," Maggie said. "Would you like to talk to him?"

"Please," Jared responded.

"It's Jared. He wants to talk to you," Maggie said. Wanting to avoid any contact, she placed the receiver on the counter. "I'll be upstairs," she said, and ducked past him into the hall.

Upstairs, Maggie cleaned the Chasons' bathroom and put out fresh towels. When she returned to the kitchen a short time later, she found Dylan clearing away the lunch dishes.

"You don't have to do that," she told him.

"Oh, but I do," he replied. "I think it must be my navy training, because I have this compulsion to clean up after myself," Dylan said with a smile.

Maggie tried to ignore the quicksilver leap of her pulse in response to his smile. "Uh...I'm going out in a little while. I have a doctor's appointment,'' she said.

"Your lawyer friend said he had some papers he wanted me to sign,'' said Dylan. "I told him I'd drop by his office sometime today. Why don't I give you a ride to the doctor's office?''

Chapter Ten

Half an hour later, Dylan brought the car to a halt directly in front of Dr. Whitney's office, and before Maggie could even release her seat belt, he was out of the car and standing at the passenger side.

"I can manage," she said when he offered his arm. But Dylan ignored her, and Maggie silently admitted getting in and out of cars was fast becoming her least favorite activity.

"Maggie," Dylan spoke her name tentatively as they stood on the curb. "Would you mind very much if I came in with you?"

"Uh...no," she managed to respond, surprised and pleased by his request.

She waited while Dylan locked the car, wondering if she was making a mistake in allowing him to accompany her. Dylan held the waiting room door open for her, and as they entered, the doctor's receptionist glanced up and smiled.

"Hi, Maggie," Elaine said, giving Dylan a questioning look. "You can come right through to the examination room." She picked up a file from the desk.

"Thanks," Maggie said, and followed Elaine along the hallway into the first examination room.

"Have you been—" Elaine stopped when she saw Dylan. "I'm sorry sir, but—"

"No…it's all right, Elaine," Maggie was quick to say, although she had expected Dylan to wait in the reception area.

"I'm sorry," Elaine said, darting an interested glance in Dylan's direction.

"Dylan is…uh…he's—" Maggie ground to a halt.

"I'm the baby's father," Dylan explained matter-of-factly, and almost laughed out loud at the shocked look on the receptionist's face.

"Oh, I see," Elaine muttered, and, casting a speculative glance at Maggie, backed out of the room closing the door behind her.

"Why did you say that?" Maggie demanded.

"Because it's true," Dylan replied easily, a hint of amusement lurking in his silver-gray eyes.

"I know it's true," Maggie said in an exasperated tone. "But blurting it out like that, now the whole town's going to find out."

"Exactly," Dylan countered. He'd made no headway getting an answer to his proposal from Maggie, and he'd decided it was time to approach the problem from a different direction.

Suddenly there was a tap at the door and it opened to reveal a man in a white coat, carrying a file folder.

"Maggie, my dear girl," said the newcomer. "How are you today?" he asked as he dropped the file folder onto the examination table.

"Fine," Maggie replied.

Dr. Whitney smiled at Maggie before turning to peer over the rim of his glasses at Dylan. "And who have we here?" he asked.

"Dylan O'Connor." Dylan held out his hand toward the older man.

Dr. Whitney studied Dylan for a brief moment, then removed his glasses, folded them and dropped them into the breast pocket of his white coat.

"The baby's father, I presume," said Dr. Whitney, as he shook Dylan's outstretched hand.

"That's right," Dylan responded.

"Well it's high time you showed up," said the doctor in a jovial tone. "So tell me, young fella…when's the wedding?"

Dylan flashed Dr. Whitney a smile, surprised and pleased to find he had an ally in the older man. "I've been asking Maggie the same question," he answered with dry humor. "But as yet, she hasn't given me an answer."

Dr. Whitney turned to Maggie. "Well, lass," the doctor began in a tone so reminiscent of her father's that Maggie felt the sting of tears in her eyes. "I suggest you put this young man out of his misery and start making the necessary arrangements," Dr. Whitney continued. "You want the wedding to take place before the baby arrives, don't you?"

"Dr. Whitney," Maggie began. "I appreciate your concern—"

"But it's none of my business, is that what you're going to tell me, Maggie?" the doctor finished for her, a glint of laughter in his eyes. "Well, I can take a hint." He turned to Dylan. "Stubbornness is a family trait, my boy,'' he said in a conspiratorial voice. ''You have your work cut out for you.''

''I think you're right,'' Dylan replied ruefully.

Retrieving his glasses from his breast pocket, Dr. Whitney put them on. ''Perhaps you'd like to take a seat in the waiting room,'' he suggested. ''I'd like to examine my patient.''

Dylan nodded and withdrew.

''Nice chap,'' Dr. Whitney commented, peering at Maggie over the top of his glasses. ''I'd hang on to him if I were you, Maggie. Now...I hear you had a little excitement last night. Let's see how the baby's doing, shall we?''

Twenty minutes later Maggie returned to the waiting room, now filled with patients. Dylan sat amid the small crowd, leafing through a magazine.

As if sensing her presence, he glanced up and smiled. Tossing the magazine on the table, he stood up and joined her.

Maggie knew she should be angry with him for soliciting Dr. Whitney's support in the campaign to get her to agree to his proposal, but in a secret corner of her heart, she admired his willingness to do what he believed was right for her and their baby, especially when a less honorable man would have walked away without a qualm.

''Is everything all right?'' Dylan asked, genuine concern in his voice.

''Everything's fine,'' she responded, noticing that several pairs of eyes were regarding them with undisguised interest.

''See you same time next week, Maggie,'' said the receptionist.

"The lawyer's office is just down the street, isn't it?" Dylan asked, once they were outside.

"Two blocks north," she told him. "I'll wait for you in the car."

"Why don't you come with me?" Dylan replied. "McAndrew said he might need your signature on some paperwork, too."

"Oh…all right." Maggie fell into step beside Dylan, who shortened his stride to match hers. At the first intersection the traffic light changed in their favor, and as Maggie was about to step off the curb, she felt Dylan's hand at her elbow.

At the contact a frisson of heat danced up her arm, and it was all she could do to ignore the response chasing through her.

As they reached the safety of the opposite curb, thunder cracked and the clouds that had been circling overhead all morning suddenly released their moisture in a downpour that caught everyone by surprise.

Shifting his hand along her back, Dylan urged her toward the shelter of the drugstore's bright orange awning. More pedestrians joined them, all jostling for cover, and in the bustle Maggie felt Dylan's arms go around her and his body press intimately against hers.

She could feel the gentle pressure of his chin as it rested on the top of her head, could smell the dark, male scent that was his alone, and a longing she was almost afraid to acknowledge sent her heart drumming wildly.

At that moment the baby kicked her, and Maggie knew by his sharply drawn breath, Dylan had felt it, too. She tilted her head back, and as their gazes collided she saw a look of quiet wonder shining in their silver depths, a look that tore at her heart.

As quickly as it started, the downpour ceased, and when the crowd began to disperse, Maggie pulled free of Dylan's embrace.

They were both silent as they walked the remaining distance to Jared's office.

"Maggie! It's good to see you. How are you? Did you get caught in that downpour?" asked the middle-aged woman who rose from her desk as they entered.

"I'm fine, Mrs. Parker," Maggie responded. "And yes, we did get caught...but we took cover under the drugstore's awning," she explained, wondering if she would ever forget those moments when she'd felt the warmth and protection of Dylan's arms.

"You're here together?" Mrs. Parker asked, casting a curious glance at Dylan.

"Uh...yes," Maggie said. "This is Dylan O'Connor. We have an appointment with Jared."

"Oh, right." Mrs. Parker darted another look at the man standing next to Maggie, but before she could say more, Jared appeared in the door of his office.

"Maggie! I thought I heard your voice," he said as he crossed to the counter. "Mr. O'Connor. It's nice to see you again." Jared smiled at Dylan. "Please, come in," he invited, lifting the shining counter to allow them to pass through. "You look a little wet. Don't tell me it's raining."

"It was, but it's stopped now," said Maggie.

"Maggie...you look absolutely radiant." Jared pulled her into his arms and kissed her cheek.

Behind them, Dylan watched the exchange and was surprised at the sharp but unmistakable stab of jealousy that pierced his heart.

Not five minutes ago he'd been holding Maggie in his arms, and he could still feel the lingering warmth of her body pressed against his, as well as the heady scent of her flowery perfume.

Jared turned to smile at Dylan. "Mr. O'Connor. I trust you're enjoying your stay here in Grace Harbor," he commented as he extended his hand.

"Very much," Dylan replied, ignoring Jared's outstretched hand. He knew he was being rude, even childish, but the urge to wipe the smile from Jared McAndrew's handsome face was overwhelming.

Not once during the past week had Maggie smiled at him with such openness, such honesty. But on reflection, Dylan silently acknowledged, ever since he'd bumped into her on the street, he'd been aware of the tension hovering between them whenever they were together.

When she'd told him he was the father of her child, he'd leaped to the obvious conclusion that the tension he felt was a carryover from their previous physical involvement.

But what he had difficulty coming to terms with was that he could have forgotten making love to a woman as beautiful and desirable as Maggie.

Suddenly Dylan realized that both Maggie and the lawyer were staring at him.

"You said you wanted me to sign something?" he asked abruptly.

"Yes. The papers are in my office," Jared replied. "Let's get that taken care of right now, shall we?"

Dylan followed the lawyer and Maggie into the office and sat down in the same leather chair he'd occupied a week ago.

"Here we are. Could you please read through it carefully, then sign on the dotted line." Jared slid several sheets of paper toward Dylan.

"Oh…and Maggie, I need your signature on this," Jared added, leaning over to drop a page in front of Maggie.

"Sure," she replied easily, still puzzled by Dylan's rude behavior. "How's Paula? Is she feeling better?" Maggie asked after she'd glanced over the document and signed it.

"Yes, thanks," he said, and Maggie heard an undertone of frustration in Jared's voice. "So…have you two decided what you're going to do with Fairwinds?" he asked.

"We're not selling, if that's what you mean," Maggie was quick to respond.

Jared smiled. "Now why doesn't that surprise me?" he teased gently. "How are the repairs to the stairs coming along?"

"They're finished," Dylan answered as he slid the documents he'd signed across the table.

"That's great," Jared said.

"Dylan tore down the old stairs and built a new set," Maggie explained.

"I didn't know you were a carpenter," Jared commented.

"Neither did I," Dylan replied. "Is there anything else?"

"No, that's it," Jared replied, maintaining a polite smile. "These copies are yours," he said, handing several sheets back to Dylan.

"Thanks, Jared, for everything," Maggie said. "We'd better go and let you get back to work."

"And will you be heading back to San Diego soon, Mr. O'Connor?" Jared asked as he followed them from his office.

"I'm in no hurry," Dylan replied.

"Take care of yourself, Maggie," Jared said.

"I will," she assured him before making her way out to the street.

"I don't know about you," Dylan said. "But I could use a cup of coffee. What do you say?" he asked as they slowed to a halt outside a small café.

"I really should get back," Maggie said. Throughout her pregnancy she'd avoided drinking coffee.

"What for?" said Dylan. "Come on, Maggie," he coaxed. "Live a little."

Maggie laughed, a sweet sound Dylan was beginning to think he'd do almost anything to hear again and again.

"Oh…all right," she said giving in to temptation. One cup wouldn't hurt.

Before she could change her mind, Dylan ushered her through the open door of the café to an empty table in the window.

"Would you like something decaf? A cappuccino, a latte or a mocha, or just a plain coffee?" Dylan asked with a bow.

Maggie glanced up at him, and her breath caught in her throat at the glint of humor and another emotion, one far less definable, that flashed in the depths of his eyes.

"Surprise me," she said, wondering if he could hear the rapid tattoo of her heartbeat.

"Your wish is my command," Dylan responded, before spinning away.

Maggie drew a steadying breath and slowly released it. This playful side of Dylan was one he liked to keep hidden, a side she found attractive and endearing, a side she could easily grow to love.

But, she firmly reminded herself, the other Dylan she'd known hadn't believed in love, at least that's what he'd told her the morning he'd left to return to San Diego.

She recalled vividly that chilly October morning when she'd awakened to see Dylan staring out of her bedroom window. She'd known instantly, by the set of his shoulders, that something was wrong.

They'd made love with a frantic urgency, a quiet desperation, and the passion that had erupted between them had catapulted them to glorious heights, sending them both spinning over the edge in breathless wonder.

The second time he'd reached for her, they'd explored each other with soft kisses and light touches, building the tension gradually, until the need to become one had overtaken them.

"Dylan—" She'd spoken his name shyly, not sure what to say to him after a night spent in his arms.

At the sound of her voice he'd turned from the window, but she'd been unable to read his carefully schooled expression.

"Maggie...about last night." His tone sent a chill spiraling through her. "I don't know what to say...."

"You don't have to say anything," Maggie answered, relieved her voice sounded firm and strong, while inside she was wishing he would take her in his arms and never let her go.

"I have to get back to the base," he said. "What happened last night...was wonderful...but—"

The word hung in the air between them like a guillotine waiting to drop.

Dylan raked his hands through his hair in a gesture of despair. "I'm sorry, Maggie. I'm no good for you...for any woman, for that matter," he said with self-derision. "I'll only end up hurting you, and you'll end up hating me."

The blade fell, slashing Maggie's hopes and dreams with a single blow.

Her throat ached from the effort not to cry. "I could never hate you Dylan," she said, her voice husky with emotion. "I love—"

"Don't! Don't say it!" He closed the gap between them and grasped her shoulders. "I'm not the man you think I am, Maggie," he said earnestly. "Don't waste your time on me. I can't love you. I can't love anyone." There was anguish in his voice, and Maggie wasn't sure if he was trying to convince her or himself.

"Dylan…" His name came out in a breath of pain.

"No. I have to go.…" Slowly, almost reluctantly he released her and walked out of the room.

"Maggie…Maggie!" Dylan's voice brought her out of her reverie, and she blinked away the moisture before turning to him.

"You were miles away," he accused gently as he set a tray on the round table.

"Sorry." She brushed at a stray tear and pinned a smile on her face.

"I hope cappuccino is all right." He straddled the chair next to her.

"Yes. Thank you," Maggie assured him, trying to shake off the sadness brought on by her trip down memory lane.

"Sugar?" he asked.

She shook her head and scooped a spoonful of foam into her mouth. "Mmm…lovely," she said.

Dylan took a sip of his own and for a moment they sat in silence.

"Maggie...we need to talk," Dylan said.

"There's really nothing more to say....'' Maggie countered.

"Look, Maggie. I appreciate the fact that you were honest with me about our...relationship. But that's my child you're carrying. Doesn't that entitle me to some say in this?" he asked.

"Yes...of course," Maggie agreed reluctantly. "Whenever you're on leave, you're welcome to visit the baby anytime."

"I'm no longer in the navy. I resigned," he announced, and caught the flicker of surprise and something more—was it hope?—that flashed in her eyes.

"Resigned? But why?" she asked.

"Because the doctors told me I'll never get back the flexibility and strength I had before the accident, and even if my memory comes back, I'll likely be assigned to a desk job."

"But...surely...I mean, you didn't have to resign—" Maggie stumbled to a halt. The navy had been his whole life.

Dylan shrugged. "I had a gut feeling a desk job would be a lot like sitting in a hospital bed for weeks on end, bored out of my mind, and I'd had enough of that to last a lifetime." He paused and sipped his coffee.

"Ever since I came out of that coma I've been going around in circles, like a ship with a stuck rudder," he said. "But this past week, working on the stairs, accomplishing something each day has given me back my confidence and made a new man out of me.

"Every morning I used to wake up and pray that today would be the day my memory would return. I became obsessed with it...obsessed with wanting my life back. But not anymore.

"One day my memory will return," he said, his tone confident. "But somehow it doesn't seem so urgent or important anymore. Since coming to Grace Harbor, to Fairwinds, I've been waking up each day grateful to be alive and eager to get to work. My life has purpose and meaning, and I have you to thank for that—"

"That's not true..." Maggie was quick to respond, but Dylan ignored her protest and continued.

"Ah, but it is true, Maggie. And now it's payback time, and what's important is you and our baby. I want to stay here in Grace Harbor and help you raise our son or daughter. I want to take care of both of you...I want us to be a family. Maggie, will you marry me?"

Maggie felt as if her heart was being squeezed in a vise. Dylan had spoken with such openness and sincerity that she found her resolve weakening.

Tears filled her eyes, and she fought to keep them from escaping. She focused on the fluffy white foam in her coffee cup, silently telling herself she'd be a fool to say yes. Dylan didn't love her...he'd told her once he could never love anyone....

But I love him! I love him! I've always loved him! The words rang out joyfully inside her head like a choir of angels singing, and when she brought her gaze up to meet his, she glimpsed the look of vulnerability in their depths, and she knew she couldn't say no.

"Yes, I'll marry you," she said, and watched as a

look of relief and another emotion not as easy to define flickered briefly in his eyes.

"Thank you," he said. "You won't regret it. I promise," he told her.

Hearing the pledge, Maggie bit down on the inner softness of her mouth to hold back the sob gathering in her throat.

"Let's get out of here," Dylan said. "We have a wedding to arrange, and we don't have much time."

Maggie summoned a smile as she rose from the table. But throughout the drive back to Fairwinds, she made a pledge of her own: if Dylan's memory returned and he found he couldn't live with the decisions he'd made, she would give him his freedom.

Chapter Eleven

Maggie stood and gazed at her reflection in the triple-mirrored dresser and wondered if she wasn't simply dreaming.

In less than half an hour she was going to become Mrs. Dylan O'Connor. The thought sent her heart into a tailspin, and she drew a shaky breath trying to steady herself.

She was wearing a pastel pink maternity dress made of chiffon and silk that swirled around her like a cloud and stopped midway between her knees and the floor.

Silently Maggie admitted to herself that for a woman who was almost nine months pregnant, the dress made her look both sexy and feminine.

She'd bought the dress purely on impulse a few weeks ago in Portland at a sidewalk sale. Needing to get away from Grace Harbor, she'd driven to town to wander the stores, making plans and dreaming dreams for herself and her baby.

But only in her wildest dreams had she indulged in the fantasy of one day becoming Mrs. Dylan O'Connor. Today that fantasy was going to become a reality.

The past week had gone by in a flurry of activity. Dylan had quickly set about making the necessary arrangements, and she'd welcomed his suggestion that they have the small private ceremony at Fairwinds.

He, in turn, had concurred with her idea of asking Richard and Beverly Chason to stand up for them. And she'd called Jared to invite him and his wife, Paula, to the ceremony, only to discover they were out of town.

A tap at her bedroom door startled Maggie, and she turned to see Beverly enter.

"Oh…Maggie! You look absolutely lovely," Bev exclaimed, her eyes glinting with tears. "And your bouquet of red rosebuds and sprigs of white heather from the garden is simply perfect. Are you nervous?" she asked.

"A little," Maggie responded, wondering if she should have brushed her hair into an elegant knot on the top of her head instead of letting it hang loose about her shoulders.

"Everything's ready. We're just waiting for Reverend Stanley to arrive," Beverly told her.

"How's Dylan holding up?" Maggie asked. She hadn't seen him all morning, which was quite a feat, considering his room was right next door.

Bev had been the one who'd insisted on standing guard, scouting the hallway whenever Maggie needed to leave.

"He looks as nervous as a skydiver on his first

jump," Bev remarked. "But that's exactly how Richard looked the day we got married." She laughed softly. "I do adore weddings, don't you?" she added with a sigh.

"Bev..." Maggie began. "I want to thank you and Richard for your support. I'm sure you must be wondering about my relationship with Dylan—"

"Maggie, you don't have to explain," Bev interrupted. "It isn't anyone's business but yours and Dylan's." She took Maggie's hands in hers and gave them a squeeze. "And whatever it is will sort itself out. All that matters is that you love him. You do, don't you?" she asked, gazing intently at Maggie.

Maggie's eyes instantly filled with tears, and her throat closed over with emotion. She couldn't speak, didn't dare, because she knew it would open the floodgates, and once started she might never stop. And so she nodded.

"And Dylan loves you, too. I see it in his eyes and the way he looks at you," Bev said.

Maggie was silent. She wished she could believe her friend, wished Dylan was in love with her, but wishing didn't make it so.

"Richard was lost to me for a while," Bev continued in a husky voice. "But fate brought us together, and I believe fate stepped in and brought Dylan back to you."

Maggie drew a shaky breath and gave her friend a watery smile.

"I'd better see if the minister is here." Bev gave Maggie a quick hug and slipped from the room.

Maggie plucked a tissue from the box on the dresser and blew her nose. She pondered Bev's words. Had fate stepped in?

Shaking her head, she reached for the tube of lipstick on the dresser and felt a stab of pain across her lower back. She'd been aware of the dull ache throughout the morning, but had put it down to a mixture of stress and excitement.

Frowning, she stretched a little, attempting to ease the discomfort, but the pain persisted.

Maggie picked up her lipstick and applied a layer, then dabbed a few drops of her favorite perfume at her throat and wrists.

There was another tap on the door and Bev reappeared. ''Reverend Stanley's here. If you're ready. It's time for the bride to put in an appearance....'' she said in a cheery voice.

Maggie nodded and ignoring the pain in her back, she gathered up her rosebud bouquet and followed Bev from the room.

Dylan stood in front of the fireplace, waiting for Maggie to appear. He hadn't seen her since last night when they'd sat with Richard and Bev, sipping tea at the kitchen table.

Maggie had seemed more than a little distracted then, with tiny lines of worry marring her lovely features, leaving him to conclude that she was still having second thoughts about the wedding.

He'd wanted to reach out and cover her hands with his, reassure her, but he'd been having second thoughts of his own.

He'd spent the night tossing and turning, asking himself if he was being selfish asking Maggie to marry a man she didn't love simply for the sake of the baby they'd created.

In his determination to do what was right, he hadn't

really given Maggie's feelings on the matter any consideration.

Dylan's thoughts kept circling back to her announcement that he was the father of her child, knowing she could just as easily have stayed silent and denied him the truth.

But she had told him, and he'd believed her, and over the past two weeks the knowledge had come to affect him profoundly, forcing him to accept what he couldn't change and take that first step toward getting on with his life.

He'd meant what he said about wanting to start a new life with her and their baby...but he was beginning to wonder if he'd only end up hurting them both.

What if he made a lousy father? He knew nothing about parenting—he couldn't even remember what his own childhood had been like. And as for sustaining a relationship? He had no memories of that, either.

Maggie had given him the impression that their relationship had been little more than a one-night stand, but after spending the past two weeks with her, he found it impossible to believe she was the kind of woman who would give herself freely to just any man.

Perhaps he'd taken advantage of her at a highly vulnerable time in her life, perhaps he was a man without scruples, a man who'd selfishly put his own pleasure first, a man no woman in her right mind would want to marry.

Maggie was a beautiful, intelligent, caring and very desirable woman, a woman he'd grown to admire and respect...a woman any man would be proud to have as his wife. But in persuading her to marry him was he perhaps depriving her of a chance at true happiness?

Dylan drew a ragged breath, reminding himself that ever since he'd emerged from the coma, he'd been relying on his gut instincts. And this time they were telling him not to back out...not to throw away the only future he might have.

Suddenly Bev appeared in the living room doorway, and behind her Dylan could see Maggie. His heart leaped into his throat at the sight of her looking amazingly beautiful in a pink dress that flowed around her and almost reached the floor.

Her hair fell in silky waves to her shoulders, and although she looked a little pale, he'd never seen her look more lovely.

When she drew nearer he reached for her hand, noting as he did that she was trembling. He smiled at her and was rewarded with a tentative smile in return. Giving her hand a squeeze, they turned to the minister.

"Friends, we are gathered here today..." Reverend Stanley began.

Maggie tried to concentrate on Reverend Stanley's words, while the pain in her back steadily worsened. As the ceremony progressed, she managed to smile and make the correct responses, all too aware of the constant ache in her back.

When Dylan slid the gold band on the fourth finger of her left hand, her heart skipped a beat at the look she could see in the depths of his eyes.

"And so, by the power vested in me," said Reverend Stanley, drawing the ceremony to a close. "I now pronounce you man and wife."

Suddenly a sharp pain gripped her abdomen, effectively stealing her breath away. "Oh-h-h-h." The moan slipped past her lips, and she clutched at Dylan in startled reaction to the pain she knew had to be a contraction.

"Maggie...what?" Dylan broke off abruptly. One look at her contorted features and he knew what was happening. "Dear God...she's in labor!" he exclaimed as he tightened his hold on her. "Maggie? Why didn't you say something?"

A ghost of a smile flitted across Maggie's face as she tried to breathe into the pain, riding out the contraction. "I thought I just did," she said a little breathlessly as the pain gradually subsided.

Dylan took control. He turned to Richard. "Call Dr. Whitney's service and tell him we'll meet him at the hospital, and then call the hospital and tell them we're on our way," he instructed.

"Come on, Maggie. Let's get you to the car." He led Maggie toward the hall.

"Bev...?" Maggie said.

"I'm right here," her friend responded anxiously.

"There's a small overnight bag in the baby's room—"

"I'll get it," Bev said, and disappeared down the hall.

Maggie was soon sitting in the passenger seat of Dylan's car. Bev appeared with the bag and put it in the back seat. Dylan started the car and rolled down his window just as Richard came running from the house.

"The doctor will meet you at the hospital," he said, as Bev moved to stand by her husband.

"We'll be waiting to hear," Bev said.

"Good luck!" they added in unison.

Maggie didn't recall much of the drive to the hospital. She had two more contractions on the way, and the time between each of them was ten minutes. A third contraction hit just as Dylan pulled into the emergency bay at the hospital.

He brought the car to a halt and turned to Maggie, who he could see was focused on her breathing in an effort to work through the pain racking her body.

Feeling helpless and totally at a loss, he took her hand in his and waited until the tension left her face and her breathing returned to normal.

Dylan quickly climbed from the car and saw a nurse pushing a wheelchair, hurrying toward them. In a matter of minutes Maggie was seated in the chair and on her way inside. Grabbing the bag from the back seat, Dylan followed.

Once inside, he glanced around the busy area in search of Maggie. When the nurse reappeared pushing the empty wheelchair, he stopped her.

"Could you tell me where I can find my...wife?" he asked.

"I took her right through to the delivery room, sir," the nurse told him. "If you continue past the emergency area. The door is marked, you can't miss it."

"Thank you." Dylan followed the nurse's instructions and easily found the delivery room. He stopped outside, undecided whether to go in or not.

"Ah...Mr. O'Connor," Dr. Whitney greeted him with a smile. "You got your wife here in good time. Put on this gown and mask," he said picking up the items from a trolley nearby. "Let's see how she's doing shall we?" he invited.

Dylan nodded and fumbled with the gown, then he

followed the doctor through the swing doors. His gaze immediately flew to Maggie, no longer wearing her wedding dress, her face was wet with perspiration, and there was a look of fear in her eyes.

"Maggie, my dear girl," Dr. Whitney grinned at his patient. "Looks like it's the real thing this time," he commented.

Dylan dropped the bag inside the door and, pulling the mask over his face, crossed to take Maggie's hand. "How are you doing?"

Her lips curved into a fleeting smile. "Fine," she told him, though she looked far from it.

"Would you like me to stay? I mean…I can leave if you—" Dylan stopped as her hand tightened around his in a grip that told him another contraction was upon her.

"Stay…please…" Her plea came out in a harsh whisper before she began to pant in earnest. His hand felt like it was being squeezed in a vise, and he was surprised at her strength, in face of the pain racking her body.

"That's the way," Dr. Whitney said in an encouraging tone. "You're doing just fine, Maggie. But you're not fully dilated yet," he told her.

Maggie made no response as she struggled through the wave of pain assaulting her. She clung to Dylan's hand, glad he was there, immeasurably pleased that he'd asked if she wanted him to stay.

She'd been coping on her own throughout her pregnancy, dealing with all the changes in her body, trying to prepare herself mentally for this moment. Now that the baby's arrival was imminent, she was both happy and relieved to have Dylan with her to share the wondrous moment, the birth of their child.

The pain subsided once more, but before she even had time to rest she could feel another contraction taking hold, and she moaned aloud in protest. It was all happening too fast....

"Breathe...that's right, Maggie, you're doing great." Dylan's voice, near her ear, was low and strangely soothing, and Maggie reined in the feeling of panic tugging at her.

She felt a cool cloth on her forehead and glanced at Dylan, who smiled as he continued to wipe her face.

Time seemed to creep forward as the contractions continued one after the other, with only minutes separating them. The pain intensified until the urge to push became all-consuming.

A nurse had given Dylan a stool to sit on, and he'd moved close to her side, holding on to her hands, gently encouraging her to breathe or pant, and wiping her face when the need arose.

"I want to push...." Maggie moaned, giving Dr. Whitney a pleading look.

"Just watch in the mirror, Maggie...the baby's head is right there," said Dr. Whitney. "Wait...hold it! Don't push yet," he cautioned.

Maggie focused her attention on the mirror, gritting her teeth together to stop herself from yelling at Dr. Whitney that she couldn't wait any longer, that he could go jump in a lake.

"Hold on, sweetheart," Dylan whispered in her ear. The casual endearment sending a warmth scurrying through her, effectively distracting her militant thoughts.

"Okay, Maggie...push!"

"Oh..." Maggie held her breath and pushed. Her

fingers were digging into Dylan's hands as she emitted a long low moan.

"Okay…hold it! Take a rest," she heard Dr. Whitney say. "The next push should do it."

Maggie was gasping for breath. She felt as if she'd just completed a marathon.

"Push!"

"I can't!" Maggie groaned aloud not sure she had any strength left.

"You can do it!" Dylan said, and at his words she pushed with all her remaining strength and brought their baby into the world.

Exhausted, exalted, she sank back, fighting to get air in her lungs, when suddenly she heard what had to be the sweetest sound…a baby's cry.

"It's a boy!" Dr. Whitney announced. "Maggie, Dylan. You have a son."

Tears rolled down Maggie's cheeks, and she turned to Dylan, who's face was a picture of pride and awe. His gaze locked on hers, and for a heartstopping second Maggie saw a look of love flash briefly in his eyes.

"Want to hold him?" Dr. Whitney asked, breaking the spell and capturing Dylan's attention.

Maggie let go of her grip on Dylan and felt her heart swell with love and pride when he reached for his son.

"Congratulations, to both of you," said Dr. Whitney. "I hear the wedding was just in time," he added with a soft chuckle.

Dylan gazed down at the tiny infant wrapped loosely in the towel. He couldn't take his eyes off his son. Dylan nudged aside the towel and counted ten fingers and toes, grinning at the halo of dark fuzz that was his son's hair.

He'd witnessed a miracle...plain and simple. Dragging his gaze away from the baby, he looked at Maggie. "He's absolutely perfect," he said. "And beautiful, just like his mother," he added, his voice barely more than a whisper.

Maggie reached out, and with some reluctance Dylan handed his son over to her. As she gathered the baby into her arms, he leaned forward and tenderly touched his lips to hers. "Thank you," he said, with heartfelt emotion.

Half an hour later Maggie was being wheeled into a private room on the third floor of the hospital.

Exhausted as she felt, her first concern was for her son. "Is the baby all right?" she asked. She'd reluctantly given him to the nurse in the delivery room in order that he could be cleaned up and weighed and measured.

"He's fine," the nurse assured her. "He's tired after all the work he did. He's in the nursery having a nap. They'll bring him to you the minute he wakes up. In the meantime you should try to get some sleep...you're going to need it."

"And...uh, my husband?" Maggie asked with a sigh.

"He's in the nursery," said the nurse. "I'll tell him you want to see him, shall I?"

"Please," Maggie responded as she relaxed against the pillows.

When the nurse left, Maggie tried to stay awake. She wanted to see Dylan, wanted to thank him for his support and help during her labor. Her eyelids grew increasingly heavy, and she finally succumbed to the fatigue washing over her, drifting into a dreamless sleep.

An hour later she awakened, and her heart filled with love when she saw Dylan asleep in a chair near the bed. The dark stubble of beard emphasized the squareness of his jaw, and she noted his long eye-lashes, lashes the same color as the lock of hair curling on his forehead.

She felt her pulse kick into high gear as she gazed longingly at the father of her child.

Suddenly she heard the sound of a baby crying, and moments later the noise increased when the door to her room opened and a nurse entered pushing a small bassinet.

"Excuse me." The nurse flashed a smile at both Maggie and Dylan. "Your son is hungry. If you'd prefer... We can give him a supplement—" she began.

"No...I want to breast feed him," Maggie said.

"Good." The nurse reached into the bassinet and lifted the crying baby into her arms. "Shhh..." she cooed softly as she waited for Maggie to get comfortable.

"Thank you," Maggie said, taking her son into her arms.

"It's a bit tricky trying to get them to take the nipple," the nurse said. "He'll get frustrated and cry harder," she warned. "Just be patient. You might be lucky. Some babies and mothers have no trouble at all," she added encouragingly. "I'll be back in a little while to see how you're both doing." With a nod to Dylan, the nurse withdrew.

Maggie, dressed now in the nightdress from the

suitcase she'd packed was trying to free her left breast.

The baby was already rooting around, his soft cries turning to whimpers of impatience, as if he sensed nourishment was near. Using her fingers Maggie gently prodded her breast, helping the baby locate her engorged nipple.

His mouth closed around the tiny bud and he began instinctively to suck. Suddenly Maggie experienced a tugging sensation deep inside her breast, like a tiny electric current, and she knew they'd succeeded.

Making sure the baby could breathe, she relaxed against the pillows and smiled. She glanced up to see Dylan standing at the foot of the bed, his gaze transfixed on the baby now clamped to her breast.

Her smile widened, her heart overflowing with love for the baby in her arms and the man close by. "He's a quick study," she said proudly.

Dylan opened his mouth to speak but he couldn't seem to find his voice, and so he nodded. He continued to stare at his son suckling at Maggie's breast, listening to the muted whimper of contentment coming from the baby, a sound that to his astonishment was drawing a response from somewhere deep inside him.

Confused by his reaction, Dylan closed his eyes, shutting out the tender and loving scene, and instantly there flashed into his mind an array of images, so clear, so incredibly vivid, they stole his breath away.

"Dylan?" Maggie spoke his name, and he could hear concern and something more vibrating in her voice. "Is something wrong?" she asked. "You've gone as white as a sheet."

Chapter Twelve

Dylan opened his eyes and met Maggie's anxious gaze. He forced a smile to his lips.

"I'm fine," he told her, though it was far from true. "I don't like hospitals," he said. "I've spent too much time in them."

"Oh…I see," said Maggie, relief in her voice.

"Well, I think I'll be on my way," he said. "I called Bev and Richard and told them the good news. They sent their congratulations and their…love," he said, beginning to retreat.

At the door Dylan almost collided with the nurse who'd returned to check on her students.

"Oops…sorry." She smiled at Dylan as she moved toward the bed. "Well, two star pupils, I see," she commented.

Dylan held the door open. "I'll be back later," he said, before slipping into the hallway.

He didn't stop until he reached his car. Once inside, he leaned forward to rest his forehead on the wheel,

but the minute he closed his eyes there flashed into
his head the same vivid images he'd seen a short time
ago—images of Maggie naked in her bed, her arms
reaching out to him, her smile warm and welcoming.

What he was seeing was a memory. He was sure
of it! But hard on the heels of the erotic images came
feelings of panic and fear, emotions he couldn't understand or explain.

Undoubtedly seeing Maggie lying on the hospital
bed, exposing her breast for the baby, was what must
have triggered his memory. But while he felt a certain
excitement in the realization that he'd remembered
something, he couldn't for the life of him figure out
why the memory should elicit such negative feelings.

He had nothing to fear from Maggie. She was a
kind, generous and loving woman. What was he
afraid of?

Muttering under his breath, he started the car and
drove to Fairwinds, his thoughts in a turmoil.

Richard and Bev eagerly greeted him with questions about the baby, and after assuring them Maggie
and the baby were fine, he excused himself, saying
he needed a shower and a change of clothes.

A little later, wearing his jeans and a T-shirt, he
returned to the kitchen where Bev had set out the food
that was to have been their wedding feast.

"So, how much does your son weigh?" Bev asked.

"Seven pounds, five ounces," Dylan told her.

"Length?"

"Twenty inches," he replied. He'd watched the
nurse take the measurement and marveled at his son's
perfectly formed body.

"Does Maggie have his name picked out?" Bev
asked.

"Uh...not that I know of," Dylan responded. It wasn't a question he'd thought to ask her.

"I can hardly wait to see the little tyke," Bev said. "Imagine being born on the same day your parents get married." She laughed softly.

"Do you think Maggie would mind if we popped up to see her tonight?" Richard asked. "We'd be disappointed not to see the baby before we leave tomorrow."

Dylan smiled at the two people who'd come to mean a great deal to him in a short time. "I don't think she'd mind at all. I'm sure she'd love to see you both," he said.

Maggie lay dozing. Although she ached a little, she hoped the feelings of contentment and joy enveloping her would linger for a very long time. The nurse had just taken the baby back to the nursery, and Dr. Whitney had stopped by briefly to see her.

She'd asked him when she could take the baby home, and he'd told her that as long as they both continued to do well, she could take him home the next day.

Elated but tired, Maggie relaxed against the pillows, closing her eyes and letting her thoughts drift back to those unforgettable minutes in the delivery room.

Dylan had been wonderful, holding her hand, helping her with her breathing, keeping her calm and focused. She doubted she'd ever forget the look on his face when Dr. Whitney handed him his son.

They were a family now, and Maggie prayed they'd have time to learn and grow as a couple and as parents, before Dylan's memory returned and the past caught up with them.

A light tap at the door brought her eyes open, and she smiled when she saw Bev carrying a small, stuffed rabbit, and Richard with a bouquet of pink carnations.

"Oh! You guys...how sweet." Tears gathered in Maggie's eyes. "Thank you," she said as she hugged each of them in turn.

"We stopped by the nursery to see the baby," Bev told her. "He's simply adorable...absolutely perfect."

Maggie grinned. "He is, isn't he," she agreed proudly.

"Dylan's still there, standing at the window staring like a proud and besotted father," Richard told her.

A warmth spread through Maggie, and her heart gave a crazy leap.

"He's a handsome little fella, all right," Bev went on. "I think he looks like you."

"And I think he looks like—"

Before Maggie could finish, the door opened and an enormous stuffed bear appeared in the doorway.

Maggie laughed, her heart bursting with love, as Dylan joined them. For the second time in as many minutes tears pooled in her eyes. "Oh, Dylan...he's adorable." Her voice wavered.

Dylan flashed her a brief smile and set the bear on the foot of the bed before dropping into a chair nearby. Maggie kept her smile in place, blinking back tears and fighting down her disappointment.

She'd been hoping for a warmer greeting from him, a kiss, a touch, something that would tell her those precious moments they'd shared during the birth of their child had forged a bond between them.

Bev kept the conversation flowing, making Maggie laugh with tales of her and Richard's experiences after bringing Kelly, their first child, home from the hospital.

"We'd better let Maggie get some rest. She's had quite a day," Bev said half an hour later. Approaching the bed, she gave Maggie a warm hug.

"How long do they keep new mothers in the hospital, these days?" Richard asked.

"The doctor said I might be able to take the baby home tomorrow," Maggie told them. "He's healthy and strong and nursing well. Dr. Whitney's going to pop in and see us both in the morning. But with any luck we should be out of here and home tomorrow afternoon."

"Unfortunately Beverly and I have to leave in the morning." Richard's tone held a note of sadness.

"Oh, right," Maggie said. "In all the excitement, I forgot you folks were going home tomorrow." She smiled at them both. "You've been so wonderful. I don't know how to thank you for all you've done," she said.

"We wouldn't have missed it for the world," Bev assured her.

"And we'll see you same time next year," Richard reminded her. "We'll celebrate your first wedding anniversary and the baby's first birthday," he said. "But we'll call first and confirm, won't we dear?" He flashed his wife a teasing grin.

Maggie laughed. "And I'll send a confirmation notice out tomorrow," she assured them. "You know

you're welcome anytime,'' she added, her vision blur-
ring with tears.

"Take care of yourself and that beautiful son of
yours.'' Bev gave Maggie's hand one final squeeze.

"I will. And thanks for everything,'' Maggie said.

"Bye, Maggie,'' Bev and Richard said in unison.

"Enjoy that baby of yours! He'll be a teenager before you can blink,'' Richard joked as he raised his
hand in farewell.

As the door closed behind them, Maggie turned to
Dylan, now standing at the foot of the bed.

She'd hoped he would stay and spend some time
alone with her.

"What time should I pick you up tomorrow?'' he
asked.

"Dr. Whitney said after lunch would be fine,''
Maggie replied.

"How about two o'clock?'' Dylan suggested.

"Sure…that's great,'' Maggie answered. "I'll call
if there's any change.''

"Fine. I'll see you at two tomorrow,'' he said, before following the Chasons from the room.

Maggie sank back against the pillows, biting her
lower lip, determined not to cry. During her labor
he'd been so attentive, so caring, so wonderfully sup-
portive. Now he seemed like a total stranger, and she
was at a loss to understand the reason for the change.

Maggie glanced at the clock on the wall for the
hundredth time. It was almost two-thirty and there
was still no sign of Dylan. Dr. Whitney had already
signed her and the baby's release, telling her to bring
the baby to the office in a couple of weeks for a
checkup.

Though she was still a little sore in places, Maggie was thrilled to be going home. She'd showered and washed her hair, and the loose-fitting pants and regular-size blouse she wore felt wonderfully slimming. She glanced down at her feet, amused she could actually see them.

The nurse had brought her son for his feeding an hour ago, and when he'd had his fill, she'd changed him and dressed him in the tiny baby outfit she'd packed in her overnight bag.

Where was Dylan? Surely he hadn't forgotten he was picking them up? It was much more likely that the Chasons had hit a snag and been delayed leaving.

The other alternative was unthinkable....

The baby whimpered in his sleep, and Maggie walked over to the bassinet to gaze down at her son, wrapped securely in his own baby blanket. The nurses had asked her if she'd picked out a name for him yet, but she'd told them she hadn't.

During her pregnancy, she'd browsed through a multitude of name books, but not one had caught her fancy. She'd decided to wait until after the baby was born, feeling it was important to see the baby first before choosing a name.

When she heard the door behind her open, her heart skipped a beat. She turned to see Dylan in jeans and a checkered short-sleeved shirt, looking a little hassled.

"Sorry I'm late," he said. "I was trying to fit the baby seat in the car. It took me longer than I expected," he told her.

"Oh, I see," Maggie replied, pleased he'd thought of the car seat, which she'd stored in the closet in the baby's room. "Thanks. I'd forgotten about it."

"Bev was the one who asked if you had one," Dylan said. "I said I had no idea, and she suggested checking the baby's room." He crossed to the bassinet to gaze down at his sleeping son.

"Here we are, Mrs. O'Connor," a nurse appeared, pushing a wheelchair. "If you'll take a seat." She patted the chair. "I'll hand you the baby."

Five minutes later Maggie was in the front seat of the car, staring at Dylan's handsome profile, wondering at the tension she could sense in him.

Something was wrong; she could feel it. The baby slept the entire journey to Fairwinds, and throughout the drive, Maggie tried to tell herself she was only imagining Dylan's withdrawal.

He brought the car to a halt in front of the garage doors and climbed out. It was as he opened the passenger door for Maggie and helped her from the car that she finally found the courage to voice the questions buzzing like bees inside her head.

"Dylan…" she began tentatively, stopping him before he could open the rear door. "Is something wrong? I mean, you seem different…withdrawn somehow. I wondered…if you've changed your mind—"

"About what?" Dylan asked.

Maggie swallowed the ball of emotion lodged in her throat and bravely met his gaze. "About our marriage—about whether you really want to stay on here…about everything." Her even tone belied the turmoil going on inside her. "If you've changed your mind, I'll understand. I just need to know…that's all."

Dylan lowered his gaze to the ground. "Maggie, I

don't—'' he began, but before he could say more the baby, who'd been sleeping peacefully, started to cry.

"He's probably hungry. I'd better get him inside and feed him," Maggie said, as the wailing from the back seat grew louder and more urgent.

Maggie reached in and unstrapped the fretful baby. Gathering him into her arms, she headed toward the stairs.

Dylan followed. Reaching the deck, he unlocked the French doors for her and stood aside to let her through. Maggie brushed past him into the kitchen and on down the hall.

The baby's cries grew more demanding, and Maggie opted to forgo changing him until she'd fed him. Her breasts were already filling with milk, and, accustomed to feeding him in bed, she bypassed the baby's room and carried him into her bedroom.

Placing him on the bed, she quickly unwrapped him from the baby blanket. Unbuttoning her blouse she exposed her right breast.

"There, there, darling…yes," she crooned as she lifted him into her arms. He was already rooting around and within a few seconds his cries ceased as he latched, like a limpet, onto the source of both comfort and nourishment.

Dylan stopped in the doorway, watching in silence as Maggie fed their son. His gaze lingered again on her pink, rounded breast, engorged with milk.

He'd been surprised, after all Maggie had been through in the past forty-eight hours, that she had picked up on his emotional distress. And he could only admire the fact she was willing to challenge him and face the problem head-on.

She wanted to know if he'd changed his mind

about making a future together...if he was staying, if he was planning to uphold the vows he'd spoken only yesterday.

And while he wanted quite desperately to tell her he wasn't going anywhere, that he wanted to stay...she deserved his honesty.

What he had to tell her was he wasn't sure of anything anymore...that he was afraid...that he wanted to run...that he was slowly going mad.

Throughout the night his dreams had been filled with vivid images of Maggie, her arms reaching out to him, begging him to stay. But each time he'd tried to take a step toward her in his dream, feelings of panic and fear gripped him, stopping him cold.

He'd lain in the darkness trying to analyze the dream, desperate to make some sense of it. But he'd been forced to face the fact that until his memory returned, until he could fill in the missing pieces of his past, he couldn't commit himself to anything or anyone.

"You're leaving, aren't you?" Maggie's voice cut through Dylan's turbulent thoughts, and his eyes darted to meet hers. He hadn't known until she spoke that that was indeed the decision he'd made.

His throat felt raw. "Yes," he managed to say, surprised at the pain tightening around his heart.

"Then go! Go now," she told him, her voice cracking as tears gathered in her eyes.

Maggie wasn't sure how long she'd been gazing at the face of her sleeping son. She'd finished feeding him more than half an hour ago and while she knew she should carry him to his crib, she found a small degree of comfort holding him in her arms.

Easing her legs over the side of the bed, Maggie stood up and carried the baby into his own room. She lowered him to the table and changed him while he slept. Wrapping him in a clean blanket from the drawer, she placed him in his crib and quietly withdrew.

Hungry, she wandered into the kitchen where she poured herself a glass of milk and picked at the leftovers from a wedding meal she and her groom hadn't even shared.

The house seemed deathly quiet. She sat listening to the silence crowding in around her, and yearned for the solace tears would bring. But she had no tears left.

Resolutely she reminded herself that while she'd lost the man she loved with all her heart, she still had his child to care for, his son to raise.

Soft sounds started to drift to her from the baby's room, and refilling her glass with milk, she wandered down the hall to see if he was awake. She stood over the crib, gazing adoringly at the tiny figure sleeping soundly.

Suddenly it came to her. She would name the baby after the two men she loved most. William Dylan O'Connor. Tired and in need of sleep herself, she tiptoed from the room.

Maggie woke with a jolt, her heart racing. She lay in the darkness, listening for the sound of the baby crying. But there was only a deep silence.

She rolled over to look at the clock and sat up with a start when she saw a figure silhouetted against the window, sitting in the wicker chair. Her heart leaped into her throat when she recognized the occupant.

"Dylan?" His name was a whisper of hope.

"I'm sorry, Maggie. I didn't mean to wake you." His voice sounded hollow.

"It's all right," she replied, scarcely able to believe he was there.

Needing to see his face, to confirm that she wasn't dreaming, she reached out and switched on her bed-side lamp. Light spilled over them, and as she met his gaze, she saw a look of uncertainty mixed with fear in his eyes.

"What…why did you come back? Did you forget something?" she asked, suddenly afraid to let herself believe there might be another reason for his return.

"No," he said.

"Then why?" she persisted.

"I came back because I've remembered," he said in a voice filled with raw emotion.

"You've remembered?" Maggie repeated. "You mean your memory has come back? You've remembered…everything?"

"Yes, I've remembered everything," he said, and at his words her hopes plummeted.

"But how? When? What happened?" The questions flew off her tongue in rapid succession.

Dylan rose from the chair and raked a hand through his hair.

"I was heading for the freeway when I noticed a truck coming toward me with its headlights on. The sun popped out from behind a cloud, blinding me, and I must have panicked, because when my eyes finally adjusted I suddenly realized I'd crossed the median and we were on a collision course."

"My God…what happened?" Maggie demanded.

"I yanked the wheel to the right and slammed on

the brakes, and the next thing I remember is skidding to a halt on the dirt shoulder.''

''You aren't hurt?'' she asked.

''No…other than getting the scare of my life,'' he said. ''The truck driver blasted his horn as he went by, but he didn't stop. I sat there waiting for my heart to slow down, when I felt a shiver chase up my spine…then it all came rushing back. A kaleidoscope of pictures flashed into my head, like a movie of my past…my life.''

''So you remember the funeral…everything—'' She halted, realizing, if what he said was true, his protective wall had to be back in place.

''Everything,'' he repeated, his voice vibrating with emotion, drawing Maggie's gaze back to his. But before she could say anything Dylan spoke again.

''I remember making love to you, not once but twice, right here in this room,'' he said softly, and Maggie drew a startled breath as his words stirred her own memories of that unforgettable night.

''And I remember waking up with you in my arms,'' Dylan continued, ''thinking I never wanted to leave you.''

Surprise ricocheted through Maggie. ''But you did leave…and you told me—'' She broke off, unable to say the words.

''That I was no good for you, that I couldn't love you or anyone,'' he finished for her.

Maggie winced as the pain of those moments returned anew. But if what he said was true…

''Why are you here, Dylan? Why did you come back?'' she asked, almost afraid to let the faint glimmer of hope into her heart.

Dylan sank down into the wicker chair and held his

head in his hands. "I don't know...I'm not sure. I just knew I had to come back," he said, bewilderment in his voice. "I sat by the side of the road for hours, while my past...my life crowded in on me."

Restless, he stood up and moved to the window to stand with his back to her, staring outside. "All I remember about my childhood was that I was very unhappy, moving from one foster home to another. Not that the people were bad or anything. But it wasn't long before I realized I just didn't belong...no one loved me...no one wanted me." He sighed and Maggie's heart ached for the little boy he'd been.

"I used to dream that my parents would magically appear one day, tell me they loved me and take me home...but they never did."

Maggie rose from the bed and crossed to where he stood at the window.

"I taught myself not to care, not to get emotionally attached to anyone or anything. It was easier that way. You didn't get hurt, because you only get hurt when you really care about something...or someone....

"I began to build an invisible wall, a wall that kept people out, stopped me from getting hurt, and it worked," he told her. "But as I sat in the car and the memories replayed in my mind, I realized I was doing exactly what my mother and father had done to me, I was abandoning my son. And I felt sick to my stomach.... I grew up hating my parents, vowing I'd never be like them, but I'm just the same...." His voice trailed off.

"Dylan, don't do this to yourself." Maggie couldn't stay quiet any longer. "Even when you couldn't remember making love to me, when you didn't really know if I was telling the truth about the baby...you kept insisting that we should get married. You wanted to do the honorable thing. That's not running away, that's facing your responsibilities head-on.''

Dylan turned to face her, a smile curving at the corner of his mouth. ''Thank you for that vote of confidence, Maggie...but in the end I did run.''

''You came back,'' she flung at him. ''And I think I know why,'' she said, silently sending up a prayer she wasn't wrong.

''Then I wish you'd tell me,'' he said.

''All right. I will. You came back because you do care, and you want to be a part of your son's life. You don't want your son to grow up like you did, without a father.'' Something flickered in his eyes, and trusting her instincts Maggie decided to throw caution to the winds.

''You came back because we're your family, and you love us,'' she stated calmly, even though her heart was hammering against her breast as if it were trying to escape.

''It's true,'' she insisted. ''But you have to let go of the past, Dylan, and let us be your future.''

Rising onto her toes, Maggie touched his mouth with hers in a kiss so light and fleeting it might never have happened. She drew back and was instantly rewarded when she saw his nostrils flare and a look of desire darken his eyes to molten silver.

A split second later his mouth came down to claim hers in a kiss that set them both on fire. She'd forgotten how intoxicating his taste was, how exotic his scent, how exciting the feel of his body pressed with such urgency against hers.

Dylan plundered Maggie's hot, sweet mouth, and

for the first time in months he felt as if he'd finally come home. He couldn't seem to get enough of the taste and smell and feel of her, and as the memories of another night returned, he sent up a silent prayer of thanks to the powers that be, for bringing him back to Maggie.

Slowly, reluctantly, he reined in the wild emotions raging through him. Banking the fires, he kissed her swollen lips, and fighting for breath, he pulled away to gaze into her eyes.

"Oh...I definitely feel something for you, I won't deny it. I've never felt this way before. It's so powerful it scares the hell out of me," he confessed, and Maggie felt her heart expand with love as any lingering doubts she might have had melted away.

"What you feel is love, Dylan. I know, because it's what I feel for you," she said. "I've loved you from the first moment I set eyes on you, and it scares the hell out of me, too." She smiled at his look of surprise.

"If you're willing to try, we could make this marriage work," she told him. "Your son needs you, I need you, and I think you need us. And whatever the future holds, we'll get through it together."

Dylan thought his heart might explode. No one had ever said those words to him before, no one had ever told him they loved him and needed him. He felt something crumble inside him and knew the wall had come down at last.

Suddenly the sound of the baby crying filled the silence.

"But I don't know anything about being a father," Dylan said, voicing the fear that leaped up to torment him.

"You can learn...we can both learn," she said. "There's only one problem..."

"Problem?" he repeated.

"It just might take a lifetime to get it right," she warned, her voice full of love. "Are you willing to try?" she asked as the cries from the baby's room grew louder.

"I'll try," he assured her, a smile tugging at this mouth. "I'm just not sure a lifetime is going to be long enough," he teased, and hearing Maggie's soft ripple of laughter, he brought his mouth down to capture hers once more.

"I'd better see to your son," she said after a brief but rewarding pause.

"Our son..." he corrected.

"Welcome home, Daddy," Maggie whispered. "Come on, and I'll give you your first lesson on how to change a diaper."

Dylan laughed and dropped another kiss on her up-turned lips. "I love you, Maggie O'Connor," he said, and with his arm securely around his wife's waist, they took the first step into the future.

*   *   *   *   *

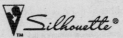

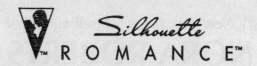

COMING NEXT MONTH

#1330 A BRIDE TO HONOR—Arlene James
Virgin Brides

Until he met dazzling beauty Cassidy Penno, Paul Spencer was prepared to make a sacrificial marriage in order to save the family's business. But now Paul was torn between family loyalty and a chance at love that could last a lifetime....

#1331 ARE YOU MY DADDY?—Leanna Wilson
Fabulous Fathers

She hated cowboys, but single mom Marty Thomas would do anything to help her son get his memory back—even pretend sexy cowboy Joe Rawlins was his father. Problem was, Joe was starting to think he might like this to be a permanent position!

#1332 PROMISES, PUMPKINS AND PRINCE CHARMING
—Karen Rose Smith
Do You Take This Stranger?

Prince Charming was in disguise, and only a true Cinderella could uncover his heart! Luckily for Luke Hobart, his Cinderella was right in front of him. But Luke had to find a way to tell Becca Jacobs his true identity before the clock struck midnight and he lost his Cinderella bride forever....

#1333 THE DADDY AND THE BABY DOCTOR—Kristin Morgan
Follow That Baby!

Strapping single dad Sam Arquette needed to locate a missing person, and he hoped Amanda Lucas would help. But this baby doctor wanted nothing to do with Sam! And suddenly he was starting to wonder if finding Amanda's runaway patient would be easier than finding his way into her heart....

#1334 THE COWBOY AND THE DEBUTANTE—Stella Bagwell
Twins on the Doorstep

He was leather and chaps, she was silk and diamonds—but the attraction between Miguel Chavez and Anna Murdock Sanders defied all the rules. The ranch foreman knew better than to get involved with the boss's daughter, but soon all he wanted was to make her his—forever!

#1335 LONE STAR BRIDE—Linda Varner
Three Weddings and a Family

She wanted a family of her own. He never thought marriage was part of his future. But when Mariah Ashe and Tony Mason met, there was a sizzling attraction neither could deny. What could keep these two opposites together forever? Only love....